Fairest Son

Fairest Son

H. S. J. Williams

Illustrations by Irina Plachkova

TRILLIUM PRESS

ISBN 13: 9781732430600
ISBN 10: 1732430608

To the Son who Forgives

Prelude

In the month that the whitethorn tree bloomed, the Queen of the Seelie Court gave birth to a son most fair. Most happy of all days should this have been, but a plague had swept through the folk at this blessed of times and touched the Queen so that her spirit faded within, and she passed from the living realm. Then did the King quake for while the faerie wilted not under time, they were still not safe from sickness or sword.

At the child's birth, the Loresman of the sídhe, wise in both knowledge and power, spoke a prophecy—

> Fairest one, fairest son,
> All together, under one,
> Kingdoms twain, now together
> A crown to last, for now, forever

Then did the hearts of the fair folk rise in wonder for long indeed had there been hope of one to call back the Unseelie, their sundered brethren, and *thus songs of joy echoed through the woods so that any mortal who heard them was blessed.*

But the King's heart still shuddered in his breast, and he clung ever tighter to the babe, for he feared its loss as well. And he bade the Loresman to cast what enchantment as he could over the child to protect him from death's reaping.

Long did the Loresman study and consult creatures of many realms and many teachings, till at last he wove a spell of a lock upon the boy's life, so that no death might touch him, until three things had befallen him. But these three keys were not spoken, and the kingdom marveled that none might slay their future king.

--Taken from the Annuals of the *Aos sí*

1

King Adoh of the Unseelie Court sat at the head of his grand table and watched the festivities with a gleam in his eye. He watched the revelry of his people who drank and ate and talked with far more joy than many of them had shown for an age. And he watched the figure at the other end of the table, brighter than any of the other host, even the golden guards who waited on him.

Prince Idris of the Seelie had come as an ambassador to the Unseelie courts, and though songs were not being sung of the prophecy, they were echoing through everyone's minds. Yes, Adoh contemplated, his people who had never cared for appearances as their fairer kin did were now enamored with the prince. They had never before, as far as he knew, wanted to return to the hosts of the Seelie whom they scorned aloud, but now in the presence of this prince they seemed to think the prophecy had already been fulfilled.

Truly, the boy—all seventeen years of him--was a marvel to look upon even surrounded by his brilliant entourage. The prophecy had not spoken lightly when it dubbed him fairest son. His lithe young body was already shaping into masculine maturity, and his sunbright tresses draped like silk across his broadening shoulders. Yet more captivating by far was the sparkling of his eyes and the bright warmth of his smile. Whether he wore robes of summer gold and crowns of vines or ashen rags and hooded head did not matter—he shone Fairest of the Fair Folk.

Without realizing it, Adoh let his smile curl into a sneer. It was just like the Seelie King to present his son as the realization of the prophecy though he wasn't quite full grown, no matter how well he'd flourished into manhood. He couldn't have waited any longer to rub in Adoh's face his oncoming subjection.

During the feasting, some of the bards of the Seelie rose from their prince's side and heralded tales and songs such as never had been heard in the darker courts. And the Unseelie listened to it like they were starving.

Fools. Did they not realize what this new king would mean? What the prophecy really meant was not that two kingdoms should be united, but that one should overrun the other. Their codes were far too opposite of each other to come into any real peace. When Idris took the throne, the Unseelie would have to forsake all that they held true—power, passion, pain—and exchange it for other things like honor, beauty, and love.

Adoh could not hear what was said, but he knew by the animation on one of his subject's faces that they were attempting to tell a joke to the prince, and the prince actually laughed as if it had truly tickled his fancy.

Fah!

His son was far more worthy of the throne for both kingdoms. The prophecy should have been spoken at his birth, not the golden haired suckling across the table.

, In far greater time than Adoh wished for, the feasting at last ended, and the common folk left the halls of their king, their bellies stuffed and their minds soaring with possibilities that they had never dreamed of before. At last all were gone save for the prince and his retinue and Adoh's most trusted council, who he knew shared his view of the night, no matter how they hid it under bright smiles.

"Thank you for accepting me into your court, King Adoh," Prince Idris said. As if Adoh had a choice in the matter.

"Of course, Prince, of course. And when you return, you must bring my blessing to your great father. I am only sorry that he could not attend," Adoh said, the words so easily slipping off his tongue.

Idris rose, his robes gleaming with their own light, and bowed low, his guards mirroring him. "I shall indeed."

"Prince," Adoh said as the youth turned to leave. "Now that the feast is over and the guests have gone, there is a matter I wish to discuss—a private matter, if you please." He cast a meaningful look at the guards.

"Of course," Idris said, gesturing for his guards to leave the hall.

Adoh watched them go with a chuckle deep in his heart. Ah, the Seelie were so trusting, so set in their ways of honor that they couldn't dream of anything else.

"Speak, Your Majesty," Idris said, sitting back in his chair, his fair face curious and attentive. Both a man and a boy. So young, so strong, so fair. Even when he wasn't smiling, a smile tugged at the corners of his mouth as if joy always bubbled like a stream with him. Sickening.

"Skin as white as snow, lips as red as blood, and hair as black as ebony," Adoh said pleasantly.

Idris blinked. "I'm sorry?"

"It was clever of your good Loresman, very clever," the Unseelie King continued. "How could these things ever happen to you when your skin is merely pale and your hair is like gold?"

"I do not understand," Idris said, his brow furrowing. The ever near smile drifted away and a slight trace of unease flickered across his features, but he smoothed it under an air of curiosity.

"Then I shall make it clear," Adoh said, and he rose in a cloud of darkness. The darkness billowed to every corner of the hall, swifter than any storm. The flowering greenery on the walls shriveled into skeletons and thorns, and the merry light of the halls fled away till only the crystals in the walls cast their sickly pallor.

As Idris startled to his feet, the councilmen leapt forward and seized him by the arms. They dragged him backwards and threw him to the floor while Adoh swept around the length of the table towards them. The Unseelie King's robes of evening lavender darkened to grey as he came, and all other disguises of good will vanished from his form.

The councilmen drew the prince up to his knees. The smile was gone now, not like a sun that has hidden behind clouds but a sun that has ceased to exist. The destruction of it sent satisfaction rippling through Adoh's body, and he noted that the boy looked too shocked to even understand what was happening. Such innocence still.

"Bring them forth," the King commanded, and his servants hastened forward, bearing various items. He lifted one from its case and turned the dagger around in his hand. The handle was carved from bone, but the blade was of iron, and every eye there looked warily upon it.

"I thought I might need to use powder," Adoh remarked, "but you've turned white as snow already."

"King Adoh," Idris said, his voice returning in a tremor. "Iron is forbidden in both our courts—"

The knife flashed down, slicing across the prince's cheek. Before the youth's cry was even finished, Adoh had his face in his hand, drawing his finger through the blood and across Idris's mouth, muttering, "Lips as red as blood. Your Loresman was very cunning, very cunning. As if you would ever have *that*. Heaven forbid that it be taken literally."

Another of the servants stepped forward, lifted a jar of black ink, and poured it down upon the prince's head, then rubbed it through his hair.

"Hair as black as ebony," Adoh whispered. "So these are the keys, Loresman? Are these indeed the keys? How well they turn in the lock." He raised his iron knife, waiting for the councilmen to hold the struggling prince still.

"Please, Adoh," Idris gasped, wrenching against their hold, tears of pain mixing with the ink and blood running down his face. "Please, you are not thinking, you will dishonor your people forever."

"Honor," Adoh spat, eyes glowing with the most unholy of fires. "Only the Seelie care about honor."

Then he plunged the knife down, and the very worlds around him sucked in their breath with horror.

The blade drove into the hilt, but as Adoh pulled it back in triumph, he saw that the prince's chest was not pierced. He stared at the knife, then thrust it in again, seeing in dismay that the blade vanished before it could break the boy's skin.

He paled and took a heavy step back. "No," he breathed.

"Why does it not work?" one of the councilmen shouted. "It cut him already."

"A cut is not a fatal strike. The locks are still in place," another muttered.

Adoh's hands rose to his head, and he turned away shaking as waves of cold enveloped him, and the sound of the arguments behind him faded to a dull roar. What…had he done wrong? Or…or had the keys been false? Had he been deceived?

Red hot rage surged through his blood. He spun in a crack of thunder, and his councilmen went utterly silent. "Deceived!" he shouted.

When the echoes of the word died away, one of the councilmen dared to speak. "Then he shall remain our prisoner until we discover the correct keys."

Adoh stared down at the prince, finding some measure of compensation in the fear on his face. He could hear the frantic sound of the prince's guards trying to break through the door already. He could smell their panic and their rage. But this was his court and they would not enter in, not yet. "No," he said suddenly, causing all his lords to look at him in surprise. "After this, there will be war again between the Seelie and the Unseelie, and the Fair King will never relent so long as we have his son. It may be a long while until I gain the true keys. Return him to his people."

A cold, cruel smile curled his mouth as he watched Idris sag in relief. The fear in the boy's face was only that of the unknown, not understanding of evil. He would learn. Oh, he would learn.

"But first—" Adoh began, and the youth's eyes slowly rose to meet his gaze.

"—RUIN HIM."

❧❦

The realm of the sídhe lay quiet under a star spangled sky, every creature and thing still in unknown dread. Deep, deep, deep down, the land shuddered in knowledge of some terrible thing, but none yet understand why that fear so chilled their bones.

And then the wailing began.

Spirits of the wind tore through the trees carrying the cries upon their breath to the Seelie Court, calling everyone forth from every corner of the wood and mound. The host gathered before their King's abode, wailing and wringing their hands.

Through the trees came a small company, once so joyful and glittering, now dull and pale. Every heart shuddered to recognize them as the prince's retinue, and every eye turned to the body carried amongst them. The guards laid the limp form on the ground in the circle of light cast by the floating lanterns and stepped back.

The great vine-woven doors to the mound flew open, and the King of the Seelie Folk ran through, his face too terrible for anyone to look upon. He fell to his knees beside the body of his son and slowly gathered him into his arms. His fingers traced, but did not touch, the prince's face.

At last he whispered hoarsely, "Bring water. We must wash him clean."

The court flew to obedience, several bringing far more water than needed, and none remembering to bring a cloth.

The king loosened his own robe and dipped it into the bowl offered, then gently wiped away the trailing ink and crusted blood upon his son's features, though not daring to touch near the boy's missing eyes. More blood dribbled from the corner of Idris's mouth, and the king raised his son's head to rest on his lifted arm while his other hand opened his mouth. The king swiftly glanced inside. Then, very still, very silent, he closed the prince's mouth again and cradled him to this chest.

Suddenly, the prince thrashed in his embrace, horrible garbled cries tearing out of his throat. He fell from his father's arms and crawled away, coughing and choking on blood.

"Idris, Idris, it is I!" the king cried out. He reached after him, but when his fingers touched, the prince screamed, a raspy terrified sound that sent even the wandering shees of the wood cowering to the ground.

The fey folk drew away in dismay, howling in confusion and grief, but in that moment, a golden glow illuminated the gathering and the Loresmen thrust through their midst and ran to the prince's side. He drew Idris upright, no matter how the boy fought, and held him fast while he pressed his fingers to his brow and sought things no one else could sense.

"My Lord," he said, turning to where the king sat stricken. "My Lord, they have taken his hearing. Our healers might fix it in time, but you must let him recognize you by some other way."

The king crept forward and again took his son who no longer struggled but quivered in every limb. Carefully, he turned the prince's arm so that the top faced him and began to trace words upon Idris's skin.

After several long frozen moments, the prince cried out again, but no longer in fear. He pressed into his father's chest, his mangled hands struggling to find the king's face.

"Yes, I am here," the faerie king whispered, rocking the boy back and forth as if he were still a babe.

On that silent night, in a faerie ring of shadow and light, where the fair folk gathered in grief, the king's voice arose in trembling song. And the very wood trembled, all the creatures hunkering in their homes, for the song was that of a lullaby and the voice was veiled in tears.

☙❧

The King of the Unseelie stormed through the woods, all shadow and darkness in his wake, and every bird and beast of the night fled before him. He had come far from his courts and he came alone, but none dared to stay and wonder why.

At last he came to the shores of a loch, and its murky water did not reflect the shining stars. The water lapped upon the rocks in a steady beat, like the pant of a beast always hungering for more.

Before he'd even reached the water's edge, Adoh was shouting. "Fuath! Fuath, come at once!"

The ever coming waves stilled, and a circle of smoothness spread across the surface. A face appeared in the water, like a reflection, though nothing stood above it except Adoh. "Yes, Master?" said the face, its voice mockingly subservient.

"You lied!" Adoh raged. "You lied! You said those were the keys to his undoing and it did not work."

"Well, it's not as if the Loresman came and told me his secret," the thing said, looking hurt. But a grin glittered in its green eyes.

"The prophecy was to be thwarted!"

"Is it not?" Fuath said, ever syrupy. "I have heard the banshee's cries. Idris is no longer the fairest one, the fairest son."

For the first time that night, Adoh felt some of his fury drain away. That much was true. Dead or not, Idris would never be able to fulfil the prophecy now. Indeed, he might even be banished from his kingdom, considering how sacred they held beauty.

"You will find out the true keys for me anyway," he said. "And this time you will not lie."

"There will be a price," Fuath said.

"Three drops of blood was a small price to pay. I will do whatever it takes for my son to be the rightful heir."

"Of course, Master," the reflection said, smiling. "Whatever you desire."

2

Three Winters On…

Peace was an elusive aim for the huntress. Ever she pursued it, and ever it fled and hid from her, as swift and clever as the hare. Only here in the high mountains could Keeva let her troubles be blown away on the wind or at least frozen by the cold that knifed through her bones. Only here with a bow in her hands and her prey before her did she truly feel master of her fate.

The stag lifted its mighty head from the scuffed snow, dark eyes bright and large ears pricked with abrupt uncertainty. Withered grass hung from its antlers like a faerie crown, and the beast's breath billowed in soft clouds from its frost-flecked muzzle.

The huntress took another breath, allowing a moment more to appreciate the beauty of the creature's life. Her firm arms began to ache with the strain of the bow, but still she waited. Let the beast's last moment be of peace, not suspicion.

Then, though she made no move to startle it, the stag suddenly bolted into a gallop away. Her fingers slipped on the string, and the arrow sped harmlessly through the falling snow.

She relaxed with a frown, the bow dropping to her side. The wind blew against her and could not have carried her scent to the deer, and her keen gaze caught no other warning. Yet the deer had bolted, and her stomach growled in complaint.

"Pardon the intervention, but that was my deer."

The voice came from nowhere, as clear and loud as if it spoke in her ear. Screams did not often swell within her, but one lurched from her stomach to her throat, and she only just caught it from bursting from her mouth. Her hand dropped to her knife, and she spun around in a low crouch.

But no one could be seen. Certainly not as close as by her ear or even anywhere near. Not even an independent flicker of wind, shadow, or light betrayed a stranger.

Then she saw it. Much further away than the voice had seemed, a figure sat among the craggy rocks, as white as the surrounding snow. She knew it was not human at once, for the cloth was too shimmering and frost-like to be anything other than faerie-spun. Yet it was like none of the fey folk she had seen for many of them danced in little but gauze and flora no matter the weather, and this one was covered from head to toe.

A long scarf wrapped around its head and swept around and behind the shoulders.

She did not feel fear once she saw it. Surprise perhaps, but she had faced far too much in her young life to allow fear of this stranger.

"Forgive me, Lord," she said, rising and bowing. "I did not know he was your deer."

Again, the voice came very close. She was still not sure how she could hear it so well from that distance, but faeries were full of mysterious powers and tricks. "This land is mine, so the deer is mine. Did you not realize you had come so far from mortal lands?"

His voice was very pleasant, bearing welcome warmth in the cold, and there was no malice or mischief in it for her to beware. "Indeed, Lord," she said with a smile, "I did know these were wild lands, but I did not expect to find any but faerie beasts this high in the mountains."

"Beast or not," he said, "don't you know it is incredibly foolish to hunt upon the sídhe's grounds?"

A bright glint eternally lit her eyes, but it sharpened even more as she tilted her head to the side. "Don't you know," she said, "that mortals are incredibly dense?"

For a moment, she could nearly feel the air suck in with his breath. And then he laughed. But his laughter did not match the merry cordiality of his voice; it was raspy, choking, and muffled. His laughter came from the proper distance, and she could see his body shaking with it. Then he arose from the rocks and came across the snow to her.

She did not know how well he saw through the veils covering his face, but she straightened under inspection anyway, one hand resting on her hip and the other still clinging loosely to the bow. Though a woman and a mortal, she held confidence in the experience of her weapons, the wear of her furs and leathers, and the strength of her limbs and steely eyes.

"Why does a mortal maid venture so far?" he asked. "Surely your lands still abound with game?"

Never is it wise to hesitate in answer to the sídhe lest they think you lie, so she responded without reluctance. "I hunt Dohmnal," she said.

And as she'd hoped, the fey man drew back in surprise. "Dohmnal? The great white bear?"

"Yes," she said. "Does he belong to your Lordship too?"

"Nay," he said, and his gravelly laugh came again even as his clear voice spoke. "Nay, he is his own master and a foul one at that. Many creatures of mine does he threaten when he wanders near, but he is cunning, and neither faerie nor man have been able to slay him. But he is yours if you succeed."

She knew he did not believe she would succeed, but she smiled all the same. "I have scarce food left. How shall I eat if I cannot hunt?"

"I would offer you fare and shelter. But I think a mortal maid would fear that."

"Do I look like a mortal maid to be frightened?" she asked loftily, lifting her chin.

"Considering I cannot see you," he said in amused tone, "I cannot say at all. But you sound bold, and your wandering this far proves the same. Boldness is not always wisdom, though. Do you not realize I might turn you into supper?"

"No, you won't," she said, shrugging her shoulders and slipping her bow back into its quiver to prove her calm. "You are Seelie. I do not wander these mountains in ignorance. I have met many of your folk and know the difference between the fair and the foul."

"Even the fair play tricks."

"Yes. But shall I else stay here and starve?

"True. But what think you of goblins?"

She considered a moment, her head bent to the sky. "Goblins," she repeated at last. "Lord, I admit I do not know them well."

"Then you will soon enough," he said, and he offered his hand.

It was then that she noticed that many of his fingers were missing, only the large and the small left on each hand. This could not have been natural for she could still see the bumps of the rest of the fingers, wrapped under cloth. She must have stared too long, for though he could not have seen her if his claim of blindness was true, he began to draw his hand away, remaining fingers curling in to hide.

Her hand darted to his an instant before he could draw it away altogether, and she felt his body jolt in surprise.

"This way then," he said after a long pause, and he turned and led the way up the steep mountain side.

Higher and higher they climbed till Keeva, accustomed to mountain peaks, began to breathe through her mouth in need for air. No trees grew this far up, only the bright white slopes under the crisp grey sky. Rocky pinnacles rose from the snow like the spines of loch serpents. As they came near a ridge rising far above them, the fey man led her through winding rocks until they stopped against the solid wall.

"Can you see well in the dark?" her host suddenly asked.

"Ah…"

"Never mind, of course not." He sounded rather embarrassed, which was most disarming, and then he rubbed his two fingers together so that a globe of light suddenly burst forth to hover in the air. Then he reached to the rock, and with a deep grinding the stones slid aside to reveal a door. The floating light whisked inside and flared, and the entire hall and room beyond lit like a summer day.

A chorus of sounds rang out of the entrance, and Keeva saw animal eyes shine like candles in the sudden light. With a harsh caw, a raven flapped to the fey man's shoulder and several squirrels scampered around his feet. Across the room, she saw the striped fur of a wild cat slip out of view.

Keeva politely stood aside and waited as the man greeted his animals, making strange clucking and chirping sounds akin to his laugh.

"Are all the animals of these mountains yours?" she asked after a moment.

"Nearly," he said, voice smiling. "All except Dohmnal who will receive no such love."

He slipped through the swarm of welcoming beasts towards a passage at the far end. "Please do rest yourself," he called, "and I shall go prepare a meal."

Most of the animals followed in his wake so that Keeva was left quite alone in the room. Shrugging the quiver off her shoulders and setting it against the wall, she appraised the chamber.

The stone was very dark, but the light hovering in the room cast a golden glow to combat the dreariness, and the brightness reflected upon carvings in the walls. She stepped back to better see the whole picture and observed an entire forest carved into every wall, a trail of birds fluttering through the trunks. Other than the beauty of those carvings, the room was surprisingly bare. It was no surprise for a Seelie to live underground as even their great king held court in his mound, but the inside of their dwellings were famously lavish. Very little furnished this room, especially touching the floor, which suggested that her host was indeed blind even though he showed no lack of direction.

Aside from the muffled wail of the wind outside the cave, everything was so still and silent that Keeva heard the slight scuffle behind the seat she stood by. She bent over and saw a full grown deer lying in a soft basket, its hind leg bandaged carefully.

Her faerie host was certainly a kind creature, that much was evident.

The sound of his footsteps drew her attention back to the passage and she saw him returning, one arm balancing a laden tray and the other skimming along the birds carved into the wall. She noticed then with interest that the birds were ever in reach of his hand and served as a guide through his house.

He set the tray on a table and pulled over a seat of carven ash. "Come and ease your stomach then," he said merrily, sitting in his own chair.

She graced him with a smile he did not see and sat down before the food. It was fine fare indeed, not one a mortal would expect in the dead of winter, especially here in this wasteland. The platter was filled with warm bread, still steaming and glistening with butter, and beside it rose a pile of fresh fruit. Such fruit could only have been grown in the gardens of the Seelie Court that were said to keep spring all year round. So this strange recluse was not entirely cut off from the rest of his folk.

She realized he did not intend to eat himself, which was a pity as she wished to see what hid under his wrappings. So she picked up the bread and sniffed it as if in deep appreciation. In truth, she sniffed for any foul odor, for she was not yet entirely convinced that her host was harmless. But her stomach growled and her mouth salivated and her mind reasoned. There was no help for it. Fey folk had no patience for mortal's lack of perception and, while you might avoid enchantment by refusing their food, you could just as easily forever offend one who would have been your friend otherwise.

Suspicion rejected, she tore into the bread with the same vim as a starving wolf. Its rich flavor burst inside her mouth, sending her head reeling in faintness. She spread some soft cheese onto another piece and gobbled it up. Though she could not see him, she could feel the fey man's amusement, and she paused to swallow, wipe her mouth, and thank him for the food. Then she bit into the fruit, juice sprinkling her cheek.

"Do you have apples?" she asked before she realized it may be considered ungrateful.

"Apples?" He tilted his head. "No, no, the Seelie do not grow apples."

"Oh," she said, eyebrows rising. "That is a surprise. They are very crisp and sweet if you find the right ones. If I ever find one, perhaps I can tempt you with it?"

"If we meet again, certainly," he said. "Now that I think of it, I cannot imagine why we do not grow them. I hope you are not too disappointed."

She swallowed hard, eyes widening at her mistake. "Oh no, Lord, not disappointed at all." She noticed a draught of cream waiting and drank deeply. Then to flee her rudeness, she asked,

"So do the goblins you spoke of bother you here? Do not say to me that you are the goblin for I will not believe it." He was tall and straight, and his coat and wrappings could not hide his fine form.

His few fingers swept back and forth upon a fox that had curled in his lap, and he shook his head gently. But before he could answer, the fox suddenly sprang from his lap and ran towards the door, yipping wildly.

It was then that harsh voices rang out as if they would sunder the mountains in pieces. The sound thundered in her head, and she clamped her hands over her ears, but nothing muffled it. Her vision shook so that she wondered if the very earth was trembling. Out of the corner of her eye, she saw the fey man leap to his feet and start towards the door.

But it was too late.

The door burst open, and the goblins rushed in.

3

Keeva's knife was drawn before she'd finished leaping to her feet. She did not know if the fey man had any weapon to defend with, but she sprang across the table and charged the growling goblins.

Just as she could see their pupils dart to her and her descending knife, an arm caught around her waist and pulled her back. Without pause, she fought against the hold and slammed down hard with her heel upon the attacker's foot.

Yelping, the fey man let her go and staggered in front of the goblins, his arms outspread. "No, no!" he cried. "I did not tell you that the goblins are my friends."

Keeva lowered her knife slowly and released her breath in a heavy pant. She had to blink before she could truly comprehend what had happened.

The goblins stood all quite still, and they stared at her with a variety of expressions ranging from disbelief to outrage. They were ugly, but not in the same way as the Unseelie for they lacked any wicked glint in their eyes. There was no denying their peculiarity though. There were seven of them and each came to her shoulder, but they would have stood much taller had their legs not always bent in a crouch, and their arms dangled to the ground. Their hide was like rock, their large ears flared like a bats, and their eyes gleamed large and dark. But here similarities between each other ended.

The foremost scowling goblin was the broadest in shoulders and chest, and he wore heavy armor on his body and head as if his hard hide was not enough. The second's scowl was fiercer still; indeed he looked ready to smash her skull with his fists. To her surprise, the third did not look awake at all but blinked at her with tired eyes. The fourth did not seem nearly so affronted by her attack, and a merry light twinkled in his eyes as if it were all some great joke. The fifth was even more unnerving with the peculiar way he glanced in between her and the fey man as if he'd caught them kissing and was very pleased about it. The next was a veritable walking desk with as many contraptions were built around his body, filled with writing and calculating tools. He looked at her with suspicious eyes through his many layered spectacles. But strangest of all was the seventh goblin who had a far lankier build than the rest. Little glowing lanterns were strung to his belt and a few fireflies spun in a perpetual circle around his head.

"Your friends," she repeated dully.

"Aye! And who might you be?" said the foremost goblin. His wide jaw was set in certain offense, blunt teeth jutting out on the upper lip.

The fey man relaxed and swept himself back into an elegant posture, waving his arm from Keeva to the goblins in introduction. "Good Chief, this is my new friend. I'm afraid this is all my fault; I had not yet told her you were coming and of no danger. And maiden, these are my dear friends. Chief, Orn, Drows, Joll, Rom, Art, and Twinkle."

"Twinkle." Keeva blinked. She knew they could not be real names, but true goblin names were notoriously impossible to pronounce for anyone outside their kind.

"What's this then?" the one called Orn asked, snorting angrily. "Why do you have a mortal maid here?"

"She needed food," the fey man said. "It's only polite."

"I see she has stuffed her belly," Chief said. "So let her be off!" He marched to the door and swung it open.

Keeva hesitated, but the fey man had already sprung to her defense.

"But she is hunting Dohmnal, and she has no other shelter up in these mountains, I am sure!"

The goblins huddled together in growling conference of which could be heard no words, before Chief again poked a long claw to the door. "Send her outside then! I don't want her gaping as we decide!"

"Aye, aye, aye," muttered several of the others.

The fey man darted to her side and directed her out the door with a gentle touch. "Never mind, they're quite soft really. I shall convince them to let you stay. That is, you do have nowhere else in this bitter cold? There are many rooms, and I swear by the Seelie King that you will be an honored guest."

Stepping back out into the snow, she gazed at his veiled face and wished again that she might see the earnestness of his voice upon his face and if it was as beautiful as it sounded. "Aye," she said. "I'll take you up on that offer."

The moment Keeva was shut outside, the goblins gathered around the fey man, grunting and growling at turns.

"You want her to stay here?" Art said, adjusting his spectacles as if it could help him see the matter clearly. "The probability of disaster is overwhelming."

"Prince Idris, your safety is our first and foremost concern! This house is supposed to be a secret, and here we find you entertainin' strangers?" Chief exclaimed.

"Oh, she is no harm," Idris returned. "She's just a mortal huntress."

"Aye, aye, and what is a mortal huntress doing so far up here?" Orn demanded, jutting out his chin.

"She hunts Dohmnal like I said! I don't expect she will succeed, but it would be a boon if that bear was defeated at last, don't you agree?" When the goblins only muttered, Idris swung out an arm in pleading. "Please, let her stay. She interests me."

"Of course she interests you," Chief grumbled. "She is female."

"Oh!" the goblin named Rom said, ears twitching. "Are you in love?"

The rest all made an uproar about that, and Idris could not get a word in edgewise for a few moments. "No, no, no," he said. "That's not it at all; I only just met the girl. Just please. I…"

The goblins lapsed into silence and considered him keenly as if they saw past all the veils and wrapping. Only Twinkle kept grinning and the fireflies kept up their steady buzz.

"Are you lonely?" Chief asked bluntly.

"How could he jolly well be lonely?" Orn exclaimed. "He's got us! He's got his animals! He's got the jewels!"

"Oh, just let her stay, it might be a lark," Joll said, grinning.

"In any case, let us be done with this bother," Drows said, yawning hugely.

"If you need more company," said Chief to the prince, "your father can send another fey up to join you."

"No!" Idris said hotly. He wrapped his arms around his body as if he only just noticed the chill. "No," he repeated, voice becoming small. "You know I don't wish for any of their company save for Father and the Loresman. They stare so. I always feel it. And she doesn't."

After another moment of unhappy silence, the chief released a groaning sigh, deep and heavy as shifting earth. "The moment she causes trouble, she is gone," he said finally.

Then Idris knew he had won, and he threw his arms around the goblin with glad abandon. No words did he speak, but the mewling cry from his throat seemed to please the goblins more than anything, and the fox yipped in excitement around their feet.

He hurried outside where Keeva sat upon the rocks, pulling her windswept hair back into its braid.

"They will let you stay," he exclaimed. "And I may be able to help you hunt Dohmnal. I have tried to find his lair before."

Keeva had not stood yet, and she looked thoughtfully upon the figure before her. Her first impression of his mysterious power and presence was long since blown away on the wind, and she felt an impulse to laugh at his childish excitement.

"Are the goblins your guardians or your keepers so that you must gain their permission for what you do?" she asked.

He stiffened as if he'd been bit, and she swallowed her words too late in regret. She must not forget that he was still fey, sensitive to insult, and not as tame as he seemed.

"I am sorry," she said quickly. "I meant no offense. I only find it strange that a sídhe lives here with goblins. I did not know of an alliance between them and the great Court."

His arched shoulders relaxed, and she knew the danger past. "It is strange," he said. "But they are my friends, and this land first belongs to them, so I must honor their wishes. And they will allow you to be my guest. You may call me …Fingall."

Of course it was not his true name, she knew that. All fey guarded their names jealously, and humans were wise to do the same. "You may call me Huntress," she said.

"That is a title, not a name," he noted.

"It is all I need," she said, and followed him into the house.

4

Keeva woke to a wet nose sniffing her face. She lashed out her arm with a gasp, but hit nothing but air. Blinking aside layers of sleep, she shoved herself up into a sitting position, and stared at the fox panting at the foot of her bed. Her heart jolted to opposite sides of her chest in confusion, before she remembered the night previous.

Ah, yes. She was a sídhe's guest up in the mountains. Though the air kissing her face was cold, her body was quite warm from sleeping under all the furs. She heaved out of bed and quickly donned the boots and coat that she had discarded, then strapped on her belts and weapons. A little globe of light had hovered gently in the air throughout the night, but now it brightened at her waking and bobbed before her as she wandered down the long halls. The fox bounded ahead to lead the way, whisking its long tail back and forth, an astonishing thing as she'd never seen the shy creatures act like a dog.

The faerie man…this…Fingall… stood before a stone table, arranging fruits on a tray with artistic talent. His head tilted as she came, and his hand flitted to the wraps on his face as if to make certain they were still secure. He tossed a peach her way, and she caught it deftly.

"Before you head out this morning," he said, "I thought you might like to see my craft."

"What?" Keeva said, biting into the fruit. "You mean you don't spend the day cleaning the house and singing with the animals?" He laughed at that, and she wondered if she should find his laugh repulsive, but found she could not when it was filled with such joy.

Turning to a small chest upon a pedestal, he lifted the lid and retrieved two instruments of delicate woven gold. These he slipped over his hands and secured about his wrists and she saw that they were formed to replace his three middle fingers. There were not solid, only an outer shell of twined design, and yet when he flexed his hand they moved with his real fingers.

"Come on," he said. "It's in the goblin mines."

The mines were not far from his cave, only a short distance down a well-worn path curving around the mountain side, and they were impossible to mistake as anything but mines with its warped wood beams and tracks leading into the mountain's mouth.

"It is here that the jewels for the faeries are found. The goblins send them as tribute to the Seelie King."

She wondered at the freedom with which he told her such valuable secrets and led her to this cave, but then, she suspected that finding the cave would be impossible for any mortal without fey aid.

The ball of light had followed them even here and its glow sent the walls of the mine glittering from waterdrops more brilliant than any diamond. The rock itself was black and crude, hardly looking like the sort of thing to hide precious gems. But as they traveled deeper down, the rings of picks and the grind of cart wheels soon echoed in far-off depths.

The voice of a goblin roared right in her ear. "Joll! Watch where you swing that thing!"

She gasped, jolting against Fingall. There was no goblin to be seen in the narrow passage, and there could be no way that voice had spoken so clearly through thick stone. It was like how she'd heard him over the wind and distance, but yet more impossible.

Before she could speak, another voice, this one unmistakably Rom, called just as near-sounding. "This jewel will write poetry!"

Tightening her grip on Fingall's arm, Keeva took a deep breath. "How am I hearing them? They must be much further down in the mines."

"Ah, that," he said. "It's mind-speak. The goblins use it for communication so they can keep track of each other here in this labyrinth."

"They speak with their mind," she said slowly.

"Yes," he answered, then added with a bit of shyness, "They taught it to me. It's how I speak."

"I see." She tried not to look surprised, realizing too late he couldn't see her anyway.

They had not gone too much deeper into the mines when Fingall, his hand having swept along the wall as they walked, abruptly paused and turned into another shaft. This opened into a small chamber and when the light whisked inside, the entire room burst into glittering wonder. The walls here were not sooty black, but every color of the rainbow. It was like walking into a giant geode, every crystal perfect and sharp and fine.

She froze for fear of one false step that would send her flying onto sharp edges. But Fingall walked in without notice of the splendor and sat on a cushioned seat thrown between stalagmites. There were other pieces of furniture in this room of terrifying beauty—a low table and a shelf. A fountain spilled from the rocks into a natural pool before draining into some hidden hole to continue its path through the stone.

Fingall opened the drawer in the table, rattling the strange tools inside, and then he picked up something wrapped in cloth, unveiled it, and held out his hand for her to see.

Carefully stepping across the treacherous ground, she bent to observe the remarkably large ruby clasped between his fingers. Except it wasn't just a ruby, it was a small dancing horse, more dainty and detailed than any sculpture she'd seen before.

"Did….did you make this?" she breathed.

"Yes," he said, quite proud.

"But—" But how, she wanted to say. How, when he was blind, and had only two real fingers on each hand?

"The faeries crafted these fingers for me so I could wield the carving tools more easily," he said, wiggling the delicate gold digits. "But they can't feel so I use my thumb and little finger to make sure the shape is just right." His voice softened. "So that they look just…just like I remember."

There were several such ornaments upon the shelf: winged griffins, fawns dancing in a wild circle, mermaids diving beneath a wave. Through his fingers he had captured his lost vision.

"Fingall," she said solemnly. "These are beautiful."

"Come," he said, leaping back to his feet, "There is more to see!"

There was something fearsome about walking into the heart of a mountain, surrounded on all sides by solid rock and trusting that the rock would not decide to collapse for reasons of its own. Some comfort came when the passage expanded into large natural caverns which surely must have borne the mountain's weight for centuries.

Fingall chattered something about the goblin's new excavation site not being much further, but Keeva paused and wandered off the path a few steps to peer into a pit carved straight down into the bedrock. The light bobbed above her head and she wished she could send it down the black hole for a better look. As it was, the light glittered off the veins in the ore with stunning brilliance.

"What is harvested from this dig?" she called.

Fingall made his way back to her, fingers tapping against the wall with slight uncertainty. "Oh. Is that one of the colith plunges? Don't get too close."

"I don't think it's that far," she said. "I can almost see the bottom."

"That's not the point. There's a gas that pools down there."

"Poison?"

"In a way. We simply can't breathe it. The goblins can because they're cave-folk."

Her pulse quickened at his words and despite the chill of the caves, sweat seeped from her skin. "Really." Ignoring his warning, she bent closer. "It's so beautiful though. Like nothing I've ever seen."

"What does it look like?" he asked, edging forward.

"Dew on spiderwebs," she said, leaning even further out. "And—" Her voice broke and she flailed her arms with a shriek.

"Huntress?" Fingall lurched forward, reaching wildly for her. She caught at him desperately, tangling in his arms and robes as she scrambled to get away from the ledge. Her heart lurched as her foot caught around his ankle and he tripped— tripped and toppled over the brink and into the depths of the pit.

His scream was not mind-speak. Like his laugh it came from his throat—harsh, graveled, and course. But the scream, in all its terror, was far, far worse.

Falling to her knees, she peered out over the edge, fighting the sickened swells of her stomach. "Fingall?" she gasped.

But when his voice cried out in her head again, it was not in response to her. "Chief!" he called, frantic. "Chief, Orn, Art! Help! I've fallen into the colith pit…please, Joll, I can't breathe! Drows!"

She sprang to her feet, cupped her hand around her mouth and hollered in hopes to draw the goblin's trail just in case there was more than one such pit. Her cry echoed through the chamber, mocking and false, before being swallowed into shadow.

Within moments, the rattle of stone under hasty feet rang through the mine's halls, and a green light came flickering, swaying in step with the goblins. All seven of them came rushing down from a shaft, their lantern bug lamps held high and their picks still clutched in their knobby hands.

They hardly gave Keeva a glance as they skidded to the edge. "Hold on!" Chief roared. "I'm coming right now." He threw the lantern in ahead of him, caught sight of where Fingall lay at the bottom, and then jumped in.

Despite Keeva's claim of seeing the bottom, it was quite a drop, and her breath seized as the goblin plummeted, but then, he was a goblin. They were almost rock themselves.

Surely it could have been less than a minute since Fingall had fallen, surely he, faerie as he was, could have endured that long. But silence thundered in Keeva's ears and her knuckles whitened as Chief came climbing back up, cheered and aided by his comrades, with the long white-wrapped body of Fingall slung across his broad shoulders. Carefully, the goblin laid Idris upon the ground, loosening the wrap about his face and throat.

"Take it all off, let him breathe!" Keeva exclaimed, reaching forward, but Orn struck her hand away with a truly fearsome glare.

"He will be fine," Chief said gruffly, though he seemed to speak more to the anxious clustering goblins than her. "He just needs a little air."

After a few moments, the prediction proved right. Fingall stirred, then coughed, and he levered himself up on one elbow. "Is Huntress all right?" he asked faintly.

"That's very sweet," Rom observed.

"Don't be daft," Art said, his entire face wrinkling in disgust.

"I'm right here." Keeva wanted to touch his arm, but trespassing goblins was a feat even heroes hardly dared. And she was no hero; she knew that as certainty. Instead, she felt sick, ready to upend her stomach. It was all her fault that he'd fallen.

"Did I hit my head?" Fingall said, even his mind-speak slurred. "Something...something doesn't feel quite right."

"We are taking you back to your house," Chief said. His beady eyes glinted in the dancing lantern light as he looked at Keeva for the first time. "And then the human is leaving."

5

A strange and silent procession trooped upon the snow-laden slope of the high mountains. The birds and squirrels had seen the seven goblins march that path many times before, often with the tall white figure in their midst, but a stranger had joined their company this time, a mortal woman in ragged furs that caused every watching squirrel to bristle their brush tail. The mortal did not merely walk with them, but she marched ahead of them a bit like a prisoner. She did not seem to think that her state however as she walked with something like a proud and offended air.

The birds and squirrels could tell no more than that, so they soon lost interest and went on their foraging way.

If they could have heard the mind-spoken battle between the chief goblin and the tall white fey, they would have quickly learned the procession was not as silent as it seemed.

"It was an accident," Idris said for the fourth time, and the firmness in his voice could have made it the final time had he been arguing with anyone less strong-willed than an angry goblin.

"An accident that could have killed you!" Chief snarled, his mind-speak always more deafening than his normal gruff voice.

"Let us not exaggerate." Idris shook his head wearily, amazed yet again how quickly the goblins seemed to forget his protected state. He could be harmed, he knew that better than anyone, but blaming the huntress for near murder was an overreaction. It wouldn't do to mention that while he was yet very much alive, the fall and loss of breath had hurt a great deal, and its effect lingered on him with a strange pain, as if something inside him had been picked out by a claw.

The goblin rattled on, his fury once rolling as unstoppable as an avalanche. "This is what comes of entertaining mortals; there is no good that comes to mixing with their kind. Mischief is their craft."

A strange accusation, Idris thought, since he'd heard what names the humans had conjured for the faerie folk. Imp, sprite, puck, devil. If they always suspected each other of mischief, it was little wonder how much harm came from encounters.

"The fault is mine," he said. "I should not have taken her to such a perilous part of the mine. And I believe I overcrowded her by the pit for she did not stagger until I was near. I will not let you banish her for my fault."

"This is balderdash," grumbled Chief. "I shall summon your father and mayhap will you listen to him."

His breath hitched, thought darting ahead to where the huntress's steps crunched in the snow. "Let me first tell her she may wait in my hall until Father and I have reached an agreement."

Though the goblin grumbled, Idris knew he had won for the moment. While the goblins were largely independent of the Seelie or Unseelie Courts, they could only contend with the will of a prince for so long.

The goblins paused some distance from the quarters of Idris, looking very much like a crop of suddenly grown boulders, and Idris followed the huntress up into his house. He could hear the stiffness of her walk, and he noted she did not ask for permission to go through his door, and he heard how his animals, darting forward in excitement, slunk to the side in dismay when the stranger entered first.

He followed her without question as far as to the door of her bequeathed room and leaned there against the carved frame. By the stretch of leather and rustle of feathered shafts rubbing against each other he guessed she gathered up her hunting gear.

"You need not leave yet," he said. "I spoke with Chief and the decision about your stay has fallen to another."

Her boot scraped on the stone as she whirled. "Ah! So you were having a conversation without me."

"Mind-speak can be addressed to specific persons."

"How nice," she said pertly, a great deal more pertly than one might have expected from a party guilty of causing a sídhe to fall into a poison pit.

Yet he could not help a hidden smile at her undampened spunk and thought it rather refreshing not to be dramatically worried over.

"I shall speak with my father," he continued, but he was interrupted by her hasty step forward.

"And I shall go for a while."

"Why so? We shall not discourse long, and I am certain I can turn him to my side."

"Fingall," she said. "Have you ever heard of the saying, do not get between a mother bear and her cubs?"

"I have."

"Also known is the saying, beware the sídhe's wrath. So I shall go hunt some game, and if he somehow excuses my clumsiness, then perhaps we may meet another time."

"There," he said. "Enough of this mysterious familiarity. You know us too well, mortal girl. How did you come by such knowledge? You have secrets in your past, do not deny it, I have smelled them since you first arrived."

The air tightened with the alarm of a startled deer. He could almost hear the swiftening of her heartbeat. Then she muttered, "I am a changeling child." And it was no lie.

The huntress was out of sight down the mountain before the King of the Seelie Court arrived upon the porch of Idris's house. Any king's arrival is grand, but the king of the Fair Folk could arrive like no other, coming as he did from thin air in a blaze of golden halos that melted the snow about his feet and raised green grass and flowers in spontaneous spring.

True, Idris could not see the glory, but he could hear it and he could smell it and above all he could feel the warmth spreading across his skin. In another moment, his father had him in his arms, one hand against his back, the other cradling his head. Idris melted into the embrace as if he were snow itself, for so rarely now did he have contact with anyone.

"What is this I hear of a trespasser?" the king demanded.

"It isn't as bad as Chief may have implied. I am allowing a mortal huntress to remain here while she hunts Dohmnal."

"She pushed him off a cliff, Sire!" Orn declared.

"We got too near a colith pit and lost balance. I fell on my own."

"He couldn't breathe, Sire, fainted dead away!"

"Merely stunned by the fall."

The Seelie King listened, his eyes narrowing as he heard the goblin's complaints and his son's retorts and when he held up his hand, everyone silenced.

"Idris and I shall discuss this alone."

Nodding, the goblins rumbled off, grunting amongst each other.

When they were alone, the king looked back upon his son. "Why have you permitted her presence? If you were in want of company, why did you not send word? I would have sent someone to you or you could…" his voice faltered. "…come back."

Sometimes there are bonds so deep that words may be spoken silently, felt rather through the heart. Idris could not reply, but he turned away, half hiding his covered face with his mangled hand. His father did not need to hear again to know how difficult the prince found the pity of his people. How he wished to be accepted as he was and not doted upon like a helpless child. That even without sight, he could feel each and every sorry stare that saw his state and thought back to what he had been before. Truly, the court meant no insult by it. But the reverence and respect they once had for their future king was now merely a sorrowful shadow to a thwarted prophecy.

"She does not know who I was and what I am now," Idris whispered. "And she doesn't care. She is here for her hunt."

The king steepled his fingers at his chest, glancing about with far-seeing eyes. "Where is she now?"

"Hunting. I think she was afraid of you."

"But not of you," he mused.

"No," Idris said, rather surprised as if he found the idea of anyone being afraid of him to be ludicrous.

"Is she familiar then with faeries?"

"She is a changeling."

"A changeling! Not of our people, I should think. Learn more of this. And if you still feel safe in her company, I shall trust your judgment for now. But do not hesitate to inform the Loresmen or me if you have reason for suspicion."

Warmth as bright as a summer sun flared inside Idris's heart. He was not sure how he could express his full gratitude for such trust and confidence, but he squeezed his father's arm with all the strength possessed in his true fingers.

The mortal huntress hurled down the mountain as if wolves snapped at her heels, sliding on snow and leaping from rock to rock until she came down to the tree line where the old forest waited. The shadows among the thick evergreen branches were as deep and dark as the lochs further into the country, and she shivered to enter a forest again. The wood was nothing more than a thick and tangled cage in her mind, full of hiding places for gnarled hands and glittering eyes.

When she slowed to a stop and the rocks had ceased skittering in her descent, there was no sound but a distant moaning wind and the pant of her own breath.

"Lost, child?" Crusty narrow fingers circled her wrist, biting in with nails.

She did not cry out; she did not attack. No, she already knew who it was even though they spoke with a voice she'd never heard. Still, even knowing the truth could not keep her from a shudder of revulsion as she stared down into the face of a withered hag peering up at her. Whether the old woman had been there all along or only just appeared could not be certain, but there the creature stood, shrouded in thick torn black robes. A more perfect picture of a hag could not be found, not with such a great hooked nose or red-shot, heavy-lidded eyes or twisting long-nailed fingers. Perhaps the perfection itself was the first hint to its lie.

"Master Adoh," Keeva began, but the frail hand jerked her off her balance with vicious force.

"Quiet, girl!" the hag snarled. "Do not speak my name aloud near the enemy. Even with this disguise I am far too exposed to be this near. I would not have come at all had I known the Seelie King was present. What did you do to provoke him? Did the first key unlock?"

Why else would he be here. But she didn't say it aloud. She never dared speak her mind aloud to this fey being, and too often she regretted even thinking in his presence for she wondered if he might read minds.

"Yes," she said. "Yes, it's done."

The hag, or rather the Unseelie King, let out a low cackle, no less terrible for its softness. "Loss of breath, prick on brow, poison apple, death come now," he chanted under his breath. Reaching into a purse bound to his belt, he withdrew a small item wrapped in enchanted cloth. Though the strength of the spell was clearly woven throughout the fabric, Adoh trembled to hold the object and thrust it into her hands with haste.

Keeva unwrapped it just enough to see the iron teeth of a comb, and then she tucked it into a pocket of her coat. "Am I to comb the prince's hair then?" she said, raising a brow. "You do know he covers his entire head? I am not exactly in his favor at this moment either."

"You will do what you must, whatever it takes," Adoh growled, and for a moment he was not the crippled old crone.

She shuddered, something within her crawling into the shadows to hide. It was always this way, ever since she was a child. There was no use in defying the king's will. He was her master in all ways, and if she could not accept that, she would perish. Unbidden, the memory of her first kill flitted through her mind. A white fawn with large soft ears and even softer dark eyes. But Keeva was to be his huntress, even then as a child, and one could not pause to consider the beauty of the creature they were about to slay. It was not a matter of choice in kindness or cruelty—it was simply survival.

6

Dining with goblins proved to be a bizarre affair.

To be sure, Keeva had seen much worse at the Unseelie Court, where appetites strayed to the grotesque, but she had never seen a meal so strange as the colorful gems that filled the goblin's bowls. They ground the rock between their solid jaws with terrifying ease and loud crunching. She couldn't help but think, as she watched in fascinated horror, that each one of these gems were worth a fortune among the human kingdoms, aye, even among some of the faerie folk!

As for her, her dinner consisted of a roasted fowl and a chalice of cream. She couldn't help but notice that Fingall had joined them without any meal of his own. "Surely you will eat?" she said, cocking a brow.

The goblins paused in their chewing and all gave her deathly scowls.

Fingall adjusted his head-covering with a nervous twitch and shook his head. "I would be more pleasant company for conversation. I will eat later this evening."

Conversation, hmm. If there had been any conversation, she had not been welcome. So with a shrug, she turned back to picking the meat off the delicate bird bones, and the rest of the meal passed in awkward silence.

When at last the supper was over, the goblins lumbered away, and Fingall offered his hand to Keeva. "Shall I show you around my castle? There is more to it than you might guess."

She had enough grace of mind to wipe her hands clean on a towel before accepting his hand, but when she stood, she said, "Perhaps in the morning? I feel in need of rest."

"Oh. Of course."

Trying to ignore the disappointment in his tone, she headed back for her room. There she would have to wait for a few hours until she was sure her host had also gone to sleep. Hopefully, he was not a night owl. So she sat at the edge of her bed, and checked her arrows, her bow, sharpened her blades, and finally touched the iron comb tucked within her belt.

It was going to be a long wait.

After what seemed like an eternity, she crept from her room and groped down the halls in search of Fingall's chamber. In retrospect, she thought she should have accepted his invitation of exploring this place after all, but the pretense of being his innocent guest was too sickening to bear.

The caves proved not to be entirely dark. Every now and then a blue light would pulsate along the stone walls. Some kind of insect or plant, she supposed. She'd seen plenty of nocturnal creatures with such lights before.

Eventually, she found his room, and a dozen of those blue lights flickered within. If they were at all sentient, it was no surprise that they'd gathered here with the faerie prince, and she felt a stab of pity that he could not see their beauty.

She crept close, heart pounding so loudly in her ears that she feared it might give her away.

Luck was on her side. He did not sleep with those head-coverings. His head lay facing away and pale long hair spread out in a fan upon the pillow. Unsheathing the comb from her sleeve, she stole to his side and bent over, the iron teeth poised to strike. But this needed to be done delicately….it wasn't the final blow; she could not be caught yet.

With a final held breath, she reached out and touched his hair. No daylight was needed to recognize the color as richly golden as summer wheat. She could feel the warmth spreading across her fingers, melting the strain from tired muscles. The sensation was unlike anything she'd ever known…certainly not among the Unseelie whom she had never shared much touch with other than a few yanks and blows. Nothing like this coursing, living power.

She ran her fingers through one more time to be certain he would not wake, and then the comb descended. Ever so softly it caught the locks, and she pushed down on the outer edge so that it nicked into the skin. A single drop of blood appeared and she withdrew the comb with a shaking sigh.

Fingall's hand shot up and seized her wrist.

"How dare you," he said.

Terror gagged her throat, and she struggled for freedom, but his grip proved shockingly strong. She never would have guessed that much power could be contained in two circling fingers, but no matter how she wrenched, they would not break hold. So she stopped, tucking the comb into the back of her belt with one quick sweep. Her eyes sought any gleam of his, but there was none. She knew he was blind, but she'd expected to see something staring back at her. In this dark, all she could see was a formless face haloed by that pale hair.

"I—I—"

"So?" The snarl of his tone made his voice almost unrecognizable. "Trying to see how hideous I am?"

"I—"

"Get out." He firmly walked her to the door and then let go of her hand. Without protest, she stumbled out, and the door slammed shut behind her.

She remained awake throughout the night, pacing in her room, clawing hands across her skin. Though unsure whether or not she'd be welcome in the morning, she did not flee at once for the hills—or rather the valleys—for the secret might not have been found out. He could have assumed the obvious. An obvious she hadn't even considered till now.

It was truly a foolish thing that she almost wished he knew her as his enemy rather than believe her an honored guest who had betrayed his trust and kindness.

The comb she'd buried under some loose stones in the corner of the cave and only then after breaking the iron teeth and hiding them likewise in another corner. Her only hope now was that he would not notice or question the minute scar at the base of his hair.

When morning came, she waited in the sitting room, all her things packed in her bag and her bow leaning against her knee. Perhaps she should have left already and waited for Adoh's instructions on how to handle it from here, but she did not relish the thought of the King's anger at her failure, and she was not sure she'd failed yet. As she waited, she studied the surrounding and discovered that it was not as bare as first impression had given. Soft furs draped over the stone seats and candles burned in alcoves, not for light but to awaken rich warm essence.

The sudden energy of the resident animals alerted her to his coming long before he ever made an appearance. And as time ticked by, and more and more animals disappeared down a hallway, she began to realize an appearance was not soon forthcoming.

Well, there was no use in prolonging the inevitable. Gathering calm into her core, she followed the trail of animals through the winding passages until the hall opened up into a large room filled with light. The light came from an enormous glass window in the domed ceiling. Or she supposed it was glass. Could have been ice. She could see the snow slopes through it, and that caused the morning light to shine in all the brighter. She wondered why the goblins had bothered to build a window for him, but then suspected that the sun might cast warmly on the skin during certain hours. The room itself was shaped in a cylinder, and all along its rocky walls were shelves of.....books.

Fingall reclined on a couch in the rays of light, all snow white and still, the only motion around him being a wildcat grooming itself upon his lap. He had a book propped open against the cat's shoulders.

He did not acknowledge her at first, seeming engrossed in his book, which was strange since he could supposedly not read it. She watched how his fingers moved over the pages, and after a moment she became curious enough to open up another book nearby. There were no words on the pages at all, just strange little ridges and bumps. She ran her fingers over them and felt a sudden sensation of a blustery wind and a lost aching feeling— she snatched her hands away for it was faerie craft of the very highest kind. Somehow they'd given him stories through feeling instead of sight.

"Fair morning," he said suddenly.

She jumped and set the book aside. "Also to you," she said, feeling rather stupid in the reply.

"I take it you did not sleep well," he said, snapping his book shut with an alarming crack that sent the cat jumping away. "Since you took to wandering last night."

"I am sorry for the trespass," she said stiffly. This was where she'd fail. Where she'd pay for her mistake and be glad of it.

"It was more than trespass. It was violation." He had not moved, but somehow he changed to look like a terrible king. Yet as quickly as that vision came, it passed, leaving him sagging and hurt. "Why did you do it?" he asked. "Why did you look?"

She held her tongue for a long and dreadful moment. So. His only accusation was about her looking. It seemed he had not felt the scratch, so she still had a chance. Wonderful. She felt sick.

"I am sorry."

"That is no explanation."

She lulled her thoughts around a bit, testing them out in silence, before she dared to speak. The most convincing lies were those flavored in truth. "I told you I was a changling child," she said. "But I did not say by whom I was taken. I was raised in the Unseelie Court."

The air in the room shifted, and he straightened in the couch, taking his feet from the cushions to rest upon the ground.

"I do not remember who I was before, only that the faerie man who took me was no father. I was not stolen for beauty or acclaim. I was stolen because he wanted something expendable and easy to train. But I was not so easy as he thought. No, I fought a great deal against his will and lived among the Dark Folk in resentment and dismay. When I was old enough, I ran. And they had tired enough of me to let me go."

"What did you do?"

"I took up work as a hunter for the mortal villages in the lowlands. I collect pelts and make my living that way. If there was one thing useful I learned from the fey folk it was how to move unseen and aim precisely."

"But why try to look at me? Did you in fact see my face?" he demanded.

"My Lord, again, I am sorry. I have offended your graciousness and do not deserve to remain here any longer. I accepted your hospitality at first because I was in need of shelter and provision, and it seemed to me you were kind. But I became afraid last night that it was all a trick. I had fallen to many a trick when I was a child. Illusions are the strength of the Unseelie. So in a moment of foolish fear, I did try to see what you were exactly. And no, I did not see you. I only felt more strongly than ever that you are indeed pure and good, and it was ridiculous of me to suspect illusion when you covered your appearance with cloth and no glamour."

"I see." He reached out a hand for the cat, coaxing it back with a rub of his fingers. It arched under his touch, purring loudly. "I forgive you then. I know what it is like," and his voice edged bitterly, "to fear the deceptions of the Unseelie Court."

Her stomach upended. Swallowing hard, she dipped her head and thought for sure he might feel her trembling through the floor. "I.......do not deserve forgiveness, fair lord."

"Forgiveness is a gift, not meant to be deserved," he said.

He meant it. Somehow, he really meant it. Without another word, she bowed and hurried from the room.

She couldn't get out into the cold, open mountains fast enough. And when she escaped, she hunted all day, and did not return until the stars had already stepped forth from behind their dusky veil.

7

Keeva woke to the smell of blood.

The scent drifted through her door from the hall leading to the main chamber. She slipped out of bed, already gripping a knife, and crept down the passage, listening for any tell-tale sound of danger. She could hear the whines of little animals and a soft wet noise she could not quite place.

Carefully, she peered around the corner and into the room which was filled with lights the same hue as a new dawn. The door was open, letting real dawn-light sweep inside along with a cold wind.

Fingall huddled on the floor, surrounded by several furry friends, and a large doe lay in his lap. The deer was panting, eyes closed, and as Keeva stepped nearer she saw the reason why. Its side was ripped open, bones and insides exposed, as if by enormous claws. Fingall cradled the doe in his arms, head bent down against hers. Perhaps it was because the deer had already lost so much blood or perhaps it was because she knew who held her, but Keeva thought that the animal seemed incredibly peaceful in the face of death.

The soft wet noise came from Fingall in strange hiccupping breaths. It had been such a long time since she'd heard herself cry, she hadn't at first recognized it when coming from someone else.

"Dohmnal," he said, without lifting his head. "Dohmnal attacked a herd. She escaped and came here."

Keeva's eyes followed the trail of blood from the deer, across the floor, and out the door where the red ribbon stood stark against the snow. Something cold knotted in her chest. Turning on her heel, she stormed back to her room and threw open her pack. Within minutes, she'd secured her boots, her gloves, her belts strung with knifes and poisons, and lastly of all, her quiver and bow over her back.

When she'd told him she'd come to hunt Dohmnal, it had not been a lie. In the occasional trips she'd taken to the mortal villages to sell her furs, she'd heard of the great white bear and dreamed of taking such a trophy. But now it was so much more than a trophy. She would kill him or die. And if she died, then it would be a worthy death.

If she died, she would hunt no more.

If she died, Fingall would live.

She stormed past where he sat, surrounded by the animals, ignoring his cry in her head, and plunged out into the winter world. The air felt sharp with ice, but the heat in her blood was far too strong for her to notice. Snow was not falling and the sky was already well past dawn, so there was no danger of losing the blood trail. She followed it up the steep slopes, losing it only at rocky cliffs, only to find it again at the top. The animal had truly been terrified to take such a hazardous route and determined to make it so far. Others had not been so lucky. She came across a few more deer corpses, likewise mauled and already dead, and she wondered that the beast had been able to catch so many.

Finally, high up on a meadow, she found the scene of the attack. The meadow was more of a bowl in the mountain, surrounded on all sides by rock wall with only a few treacherous paths leading in and out. A few straggling trees and remnants of grass rose up from the snow-slicked ground. And everywhere, absolutely everywhere, lay dead dear. Bucks, does, yearlings. It wasn't merely a hunt. It was a massacre.

She perched on the outcropping cliff, gripping tight onto the stone as her vision spun. What kind of animal did this? It was not natural behavior. It was the act of ancient evil, grown fat on the blood of innocents. The white bear was no different than Adoh. If she could not kill her master, then she would at least see this creature harmed no more.

Gritting her teeth, she crept along the edge above the meadow, looking for any trail of where Dohmnal might have gone. There, a smashed and red path across the snow led higher up the mountain. The wicked old beast had taken a prize after all. Her bow was in her hand by now, and she took great care to keep her fur-padded steps soft on the stone and snow.

The mountain this far up was truly dangerous, the snow obscuring the jagged rocks, and the exposed rocks all covered in ice. She only hoped that the swift wind would keep her scent away from the bear and not sweep it straight to his nose. The keen of the wind's cry disabled her sense of hearing any sign of the monster.

And then suddenly, she was staring at his cave. The opening was so far back under an icicle-strung ledge that the dark mouth was nearly lost in shadow. But the bones and scarlet stains declared it the lair without a doubt.

She climbed up a little higher on the rocks opposite the cave and considered. She did not think he would able to claw up to where she crouched, but if he did she had a quick path up to the top and level ground. Now there was simply the matter of waiting. Except, waiting could prove useless. He'd eaten his fill and could very likely not come back out for days. Yet only the very foolish would consider confronting a bear in its den.

She dug into the packs at her side until she found a long strip of green bark and a ribbon of cloth, which she began wrapping tightly around an arrowhead. If she could fire a smoking arrow into the cave, it might be enough to flush the bear out. And while he was disoriented, she could take the shot. It took her several minutes to make sure the binding was secure before she reached for the tinderbox.

A deep growl shook the ground beneath her.

She froze, stomach tying in a knot. No. No, he could not have come out of the cave without her noticing. Unless, perhaps, he had never been in there.

Slowly, her gaze flicked down to stare at the great white bear below.

Dohmnal was giant. Far larger than she'd guessed, he was thick with muscle and matted fur. The stubs of arrows rose from his haunches, and scars left patches of his skin bare. His muzzle was nocked with deep rivulets, curling back the skin even further than an ordinary snarl to show the terrible teeth barred her way. A deep wet huff shuddered through his body, and a red glint shone in his dark eyes.

She wasn't high enough. She leapt even as his muscles gathered, and her hands caught the next ledge, swinging her just out of reach of his rearing swipe. His snarl shook every bone in her body and she collapsed upon the top of the cliff. He reared up again, clawing at the rock-face and sending gravel scattering.

Move, run, flee. Terror was pleading for her to escape, but she had not come this far to run away. Rolling onto her knees, she snatched an arrow from her quiver and shot it straight down at the furious beast. But the shot was wild and the bear more so, and it only glanced off its neck.

Before she could aim a second time, Dohmnal leapt and came so near the top that she flung herself backwards. No, this was too close. Her element of surprise was lost; it was she who was taken unawares and she was not prepared to take on a monster of this size in close combat.

Turning, she raced across the jagged ledges, hoping to lose him in the maze of rocky peaks. Her boots were made for the sharp edges and slick surfaces so even at that frantic pace she found each step secure. Running was a part of hunting, and she was adept at crossing the roughest terrains.

The rocky palisades descended back into snowy slopes, and she hit the iced shell with a crunch. Once she was sure she'd lost the bear's trail, she could circle back and try—

Dohmnal's roar thundered, and she spun to see him charging around a corner of the mountain towards her. But—the wind was not blowing the way of her scent—she'd surely gone out of sight—

This was his mountain. He was the king of the snowy peaks, a cruel cunning king. No one came up this far without his knowledge and no one ever left.

There was nothing before her but a steep snow slope, and for a moment she considered charging or sliding down it for bears could not move as fast downhill, but she wasn't at all sure she wouldn't end up somersaulting out of control and finish with a broken neck. So she turned and raced back to the palisades. There were chasms in them, wide enough that she could fit in, narrow enough that he could not follow.

She squeezed in, almost ripping her quiver from her back. Once far enough inside, she found room to wrench around and face the opening. The bear was tearing at the rock with his teeth and claws, making so much rubble fall away that she did not feel altogether safe. With some strain, she managed to pull off her bow and string an arrow to the notch. This time, she would be steady. This time she would breathe and let her heartbeat slow and her eyes focus. This time, she would not miss.

The bear shoved his face into the chasm again, mouth wide and slavering, and she shot.

The arrow plunged into its neck just as it snapped its mouth shut. It reeled back, clawed hard at the arrow and broke it, then leapt to the top of the rocks with a heave. She ducked just in time to miss being swiped with its paw as it reached down from up above.

She'd hunted bears before. This one was nothing like those other bears.

"HUNTRESS!"

She screamed as Fingall's voice shouted in her head.

"What, what, where are you?" she gasped, forgetting that as well as she could hear him, he wouldn't hear her.

But Dohmnal gave a confused growl from up above and she looked back to see him swiping at his head and ears. With a huff and then a roar, he left her chasm, and the sound of him faded into the distance.

A silhouette suddenly filled up the light of the chasm entrance, and she almost screamed again before recognizing Fingall.

"Fool girl!" he cried. "You actually have attacked Dohmnal!"

"What else did you think I was doing?" she snapped, half in anger, half in fear.

"Come on!" he said, reaching out a hand. "I spoke to him and so he knows someone else is on the mountain, but he hasn't found me yet. Let's get out of here."

"I shot him," she whispered, scrambling forward. "It should have been a fatal hit."

"His skin is tough as iron with as long as he's lived," he said, helping her out. "Not even faerie-made weapons have pierced his hide."

"I'll go for the eye then," she said.

Before he could answer, they heard Dohmnal's growling roar, coming near again. Fingall gripped her hands for a few seconds and then quietly said, "I will give you the opening you need."

A startled protest began to flutter from her lips, but he was already gone, moving much faster across the snow than she'd ever been able. The white on white was almost flawlessly matched and he appeared little more than a ghost.

But Dohmnal saw him nevertheless and came charging out of the rocks in pursuit. Keeva followed in his wake, heading for the high ground where she could get the best angle. She had to be fast; faerie or not, there was no telling how long Fingall could keep away from the bear.

"Stay there, I'll bring him back around." His voice was firm in her mind, not carrying any of the breath he must have been panting.

She skidded to the end of a ledge and crouched, balancing the bow on her knee until she was ready to lift, pull, and fire with the max of her strength. Ice on the wind nipped at her cheeks and she squinted in the brightness of the snow. But her mind was calm now, honed and ready for the kill.

Fingall came fleeting back, the bear hot on his trail, and then just as they came in perfect range for her, he ground to a stop and threw himself around to face the beast. Dohmnal lurched to a stop in surprise and rose up on his haunches, releasing a hot breath into the frozen air.

And for just a moment, Keeva hesitated as she drew the bow taunt. She wondered if the bear would show reverence and mercy to him as all the other animals did. She wondered if its heart was truly hard as stone. She wondered if perhaps there was a little love left in it.

"Huntress…?" Fingall's voice held fear.

Dohmnal lurched back onto all fours and struck him with a giant paw.

The faerie flew backwards, crunching through the ice layer. The bear lunged towards him, teeth bared and eyes filled with wicked light—

And Keeva let the arrow fly.

The light in the wicked eyes winked out, stifled by the shaft embedded up to the feathered end. The great white bear stumbled, then heaved to the side, and collapsed.

Leaping from the ledge, she sank into the snow and hurried over to Fingall, who was just starting to sit up with a bit of a struggle. He held a hand to his ribs and his wrappings were a bit lopsided, though still covering.

"I'm sorry!" she gasped. "I—I thought for a moment he wouldn't hurt you."

"Well." He gingerly prodded his side and flinched. "I've learned not to expect mercy from evil old beasts. But—" his tone lifted in wonder. "You shot him. He's actually dead. Well done, Huntress! Your aim is true."

"I should have never hesitated," she ground out. "You were beyond reckless to stand there like that and chance me missing."

"It's not like I was afraid of dying," he said, the smirk clear in his words.

Ha, how did he know he hadn't run out of his luck yet! Wait. Did he know his keys? Was it something he was told beforehand or something he felt? Maybe he just assumed he was safe.

Before she could think it all through, a loud racket of snarls and cries and clashing metal came raging up the hill towards them, the sound only a little ahead of its source—seven angry goblins, waving their weapons like fiends.

"How'd they—?" she began.

"I called them as soon as I took off after you. Took them long enough to get out of their caves."

The goblins reached them, bristling for battle, but they found the threat quite taken care of. So they stood and stared gaping at the dead body of Dohmnal, and then they gaped at Keeva and Fingall. And then they began talking all at once, so that any word was impossible to understand. But the tone was clear, and Keeva began to smile as they hefted the bear between their stony arms and cheered loud and lustily.

The goblins not carrying the bear scooped Keeva and Fingall onto their shoulders, and the huntress gasped in surprise, clinging to the rock head beneath her. But the perch seemed solid enough, and so she laughed along with the prince as the goblins carried them down the triumphant path home.

8

When she woke in the morning, the glowing memories of her triumph and the celebrations of the night before were suddenly stamped out by cruel and bleak reality.

Dohmnal was dead, and she no longer had an excuse to stay. The bear was not her true prey.

Groaning, she rubbed her hands down her face until the skin stretched white before color returned in a blotchy, unflattering red. She didn't want to think about her true mission. She wanted to think of how perfect last night had felt as the goblins had skinned the bear and stretched out its fur to dry. What a trophy it was to see, filling her with conflicting pride and guilt. In a way, it was sad that such a mighty creature was felled, but at least the mountains were safer now.

Her success had won her the favor of the goblins at last, and the feast they had hosted was something she'd always remember. To Keeva's relief, they had not eaten Dohmnal. He was too old and extent of his wickedness was considered a curse upon his flesh. The goblins themselves still ate their living jewels, but they had prepared juicy meats and roasted vegetables in such abundance that the majority of it had to be fed to the pets even after Keeva's stomach was filled to bursting.

But the memory of the warmth and camaraderie she had felt last night was false and fleeting, and the present problem at hand reared its ugly head for attention.

Loss of breath, prick on brow, poison apple, death come now.

The first two were complete, but where on earth up here was she supposed to find an apple? Adoh had not given her any instruction on that, and the best option she could see was journeying back down to the human lands and finding one in the market.

"Huntress?"

Somehow, it never ceased to startle her when he called out to her. It wasn't only because he had a habit of coming up on her without warning or that his mind-speak was always so close and clear. She always wondered if she'd been found out.

She jumped to her feet and faced him. He stood in the doorway and when she cleared her throat, he took a few steps in. If this was about her needing to leave now that Dohmnal was dealt with, she had no idea how to reply.

"My Lord…"

"I wish you to see me."

Keeva froze, back stiffening. "That is not necessary, my Lord."

"It is to me," he said, and she could hear how husky his breath was even muffled behind the wraps. "You have been my guest, and you are now my friend. I trusted you, and we defeated Dohmnal together. I want you to know that you can trust me. If you need to see my face for that, then so be it."

She opened her mouth, then closed it. If her words were scarce before, they were non-existent now, and she could do nothing but watch him.

He hesitated. "There is another thing," he said. "Fingall is not my true name."

"I didn't expect you to give me your real name."

"I would like you to have it. It will help you understand. I …I am Idris. Prince of the Seelie Court."

She wondered if she could pull off acting surprised. For the longest time, she'd feared letting her knowledge of his real name and identity slip. It would be a relief not to pretend anymore. So she answered, "I thought as much."

"Did you?" He straightened in surprise.

"I had heard of the tragedy that befell the Seelie Prince," she said. "During my days among the foul folk. Eventually I wondered if that was what you were hiding beneath all those wrappings."

He nodded, shoulders slumping. "Well. Now you will be able to see for yourself."

Slowly, he slipped each glove off his hand. The three middle fingers were no more than scarred nubs along his knuckles. Those hands trembled as they reached up to the wide scarf and began to unwind it. The lower half of his face was unveiled first. A refined jaw and chin, a perfectly formed mouth, beautiful even though twisted to the side with agitation. The wrap dropped to the ground in a puddle of white. He grasped the tight cap encasing the upper half of his face and yanked it savagely off. The sunshine hair she had touched swept free, tumbling across his shoulders. The silken shining strands were a strange frame for the ruin of his features.

And such a ruin it was. His eyes were missing, as she had known they would be. Scars ran rivulets from the empty hollows across his brow and upper cheeks. His graceful pointed ears were nicked as if by wild strokes of a knife. And somewhere behind those beautiful lips, she knew there was no tongue.

The contrast of what beauty had once existed and what scarring marred it now was not easy to look at, that was true. She was glad he couldn't see, couldn't see any dismay flicker across her face.

Adoh. Adoh had done this to him. Taken his sight, taken his speech, and marred his touch. Monster.

That was it then. The prophecy of the Fairest One had been thwarted.

Yet, she found herself compelled to keep staring at him, to look past the puckered markings. It wasn't a mere matter of focusing only what good features still remained to him. It was because…this was him…the kind man who had given her so much. That was all that really mattered. And the more she thought of him, the less repulsive his face became.

Taking a deep breath, she reached out and ran a finger down a jagged scar across his cheek. "Does anything still hurt?"

"No."

She'd already seen how the goblins could speak without their mouths moving, but that hardly helped hearing his voice while his lips remained still.

"Is this all the damage?"

"Yes. My enemy tried to take my hearing by pouring hot oil down my ears, but my father's healers were able to fix that."

"Why do you cover your face?"

"Who would want to look at it?" he said, with a small growl.

"I've seen hideous faces, believe me. Yours is not one of them." It couldn't be. Not when it belonged to someone with a heart like his.

"The scars make my people sad."

"But your smile would lift their spirits, would it not? Why hide that smile?"

He paused, folding his arms and tapping a foot on the ground in a nervous cadence. "I forget to smile anymore when I am among them."

"Then don't forget anymore. Smile because they love you. Smile because you're alive. Smile because you can."

"You have not even seen me smile," he said, but even as the words slipped from his mind, his mouth twitched and curved in a bashful grin.

"There, see," she said, tapping him on the chin. "It is a beautiful smile."

"There is a festival among my people this upcoming full moon," he blurted.

She stepped back, hesitating, but he went on ahead, blind to the fear that leapt onto her face.

"I promised my father I would come. And I would be honored if you would accompany me. You have accepted me before you ever saw my face, and now that you have, you accept me still. You have given me confidence that I still may live in strength even though my enemies sought to ruin me. I am not..." His voice halted, almost as if he had to swallow. "I am not ashamed when I am with you."

She stared. This was unexpected. She'd hoped to find some reason to stay now that the bear was dead, and here it was, but now that it had come, she did not want it. Or perhaps she did want it...for an entirely different reason. But the invitation twisted her gut in more ways than just confusion. "I...have attended fey festivals before, my lord. They did not settle well with me."

His head twitched in swift understanding. "Ah. Yes. The Unseelie Court is given to unchecked passion, most of it dark. Such has not been tolerated in my father's court for many generations. It is written that such passions are only for those trothed to one another. Even if it were not so, you would be safe by my side."

Scuffing her boot across the ground, she lingered in reply. Going among the Fair Folk would surely be a risk. Would they smell the treachery on her even when Idris could not? But if she did not go, there was no reason to remain…

"My name is Keeva." It is not what she had intended to say. All that she had meant to come out was a simple acceptance of his invitation. But now that the name was out, there was no taking it back.

"Keeva…"

A tingle pattered up her spine at how he spoke it. Like it was something special, precious, honorable. She knew then she did not regret giving it, no matter what else might happen. She inhaled, closing her eyes, and treasured the sound away in memory. "I will come as your guest," she said.

9

The night came all too soon. When the moon began to rise in a glorious golden glow over the dark mountain peaks, a strange procession wound down from the snowy heights to the forest floors. Goblins did not usually leave their mountains, but when they did, they could be clearly heard, for they marched in time and sang loud songs in a strange language that told of ancient tales and fabled treasures. They carried litters upon their shoulders and upon these were statues carved from shining jewels worth kingdoms of men.

In the midst of the goblins walked the pair who truly made the procession strange (for in these parts, goblins were really nothing to remark about).

Idris still wore his white robes and coverings, and Keeva still wore her huntress attire. He had assured her they would be given proper clothing at the festivities and that the transformation was part of the ceremonies.

Since they'd started walking, they had not exchanged a word and somehow a sphere of snowflake silence enveloped them despite the raucous goblin ballads. Idris had looped his arm through hers, and she was not sure if it was to assist him in walking or if was purely the courtesy of a gentleman. Either way, being so close to him both pleased and frightened her. She could not help but notice as she matched his stride that he walked like a king.

The deeper down they plunged, the thicker the forest became, and all the snow melted away. Soon even the regular chill of nature was replaced by something warm and magical. They were walking a faerie path, she knew, and her fingers curled tight into Idris's arm. As a rule, she avoided faerie paths as much as she could. A mortal straying upon them would find only death. But she was no mere mortal, and she was not alone now. Here, by this strange prince's side, she was safe.

The trees grew taller and straighter till they soon appeared to be pillars of a grand castle, and the forest path itself widened into a carpet laden with golden moss and small white flowers. Glowing lights, brighter and more enduring than fireflies, began to wink at them through the shadows. The murmuring of the wind tuned to the melodies of music.

A thrill began to clasp her heart. She had always seen only one side of the Faerie before—the shadows and horrors of the Unseelie Court. But there was so much more. There was beauty and joy and wonder in the land of light. True, she knew the

Seelie would always be wild and thus not quite safe, but at the heart of things, at the essence of their being, there was good.

"The prince! The prince! Our prince has returned to us! He has come, he has come, at last!" The voices rose in the wood around them, in varying cadences of excitement. A powerful energy rushed ahead of them, carrying the declaration to all.

And then the mound of the Seelie Court rose before them. On the outside it was little more than a hill covered in bracken and moss with a door in the side of it, a warm light spilling out through the open entry. But as they marched through that door and into the golden light, the world changed, becoming larger on the inside than could ever be dreamed.

A different kind of forest grew here, one that sparkled with silver and gold leaves in a thousand lights, all chiming in a song felt more often than heard. The roof overhead was painted in so lifelike of murals that it appeared to have no end to its height, and she wondered if in fact it was a whole other real world looking down upon them. Fauns and nymphs danced around them, joining their ever-expanding procession as they covered leagues in a single stride.

One second, Keeva was clinging to Idris's arm in frantic determination to not lose hold and be lost forever in the Seelie Court, and the next second, they all stood before the throne of the Seelie King.

She knew she was gaping, and she didn't care. The arches, the dais, the steps, and the throne itself were all entwined together in intricate pattern of golden wood that dazzled and confused the eye. But the movement of the craftsmanship led one's attention straight to the center and the king.

He was very beautiful, and she wondered exactly how Idris could have eclipsed him. She would have liked to study him much longer, but he was perhaps her most dangerous enemy here, and so she let her gaze drop lower. She noticed then the man in robes upon the second stair and by his aura of wisdom alone she knew him to be the Loresman. So much she had been told by Adoh in her training and now it was all alive and standing in front of her eyes.

It terrified her.

"I have come, Father," Idris said, his voice ringing to every corner. "And I have brought my friend and guest, the huntress Keeva who slew Dohmnal, the monster of the mountains. Keeva, my father…Deorsa of the Fair Folk."

His father rose, in that moment seeming as tall and mighty as a mountain. But when he looked upon his son, there was nothing fearful in his gaze, only tenderness. "I welcome any friend of yours to the court, my son. And I am glad you have returned to us." He stepped down and embraced Idris, then turned to Keeva with a look of curiosity.

She quickly bowed, unwilling to meet his eye and unwilling to do anything such as take his hand for he would surely feel the wild traitorous pulse of her blood.

"I am indebted to you for the happiness you have given my son," he said solemnly. "Tonight, may you find joy in the feasting. Ladies Fair, please see that she is given every honor we may bestow."

With those words, Keeva found herself being rushed away in a crowd of women who were not all quite woman but also part breeze and leaf. She tried to look back, only just glimpsing the sight of Idris walking away, his father's arm wrapped around his shoulder. The strength in the fey women's pull was hopeless to resist, so she let herself get herded through strange halls and into a dressing room.

Afterwards she was never quite sure whether she'd changed clothes or if they literally changed what she was wearing, but in little time, she was wearing a grey gown, sparkling and soft as morning mist, and seated before a waterfall mirror while the women around her arranged her hair and appearance.

She kept very still throughout it all and tried not to look directly at any of the sídhe maidens, but she could feel them peering at her. Little wonder why. No doubt they were wild with curiosity as to why their fey prince would bring a mortal woman as his guest. As humans went, Keeva had learned she was pretty enough, but by faerie standards, which were as lavish and exotic as orchids, she suspected she'd be viewed as rather plain and uninteresting.

There was one particular gaze that burned deep, and she at last had to look for its source. She found it from a tall woman standing aside who had not taken part in the preening, but glared at Keeva as if her life depended upon it. It was not a glare of jealousy, but of deep suspicion.

"Who is our prince to you?" the woman asked abruptly, and all the idle chatter in the room halted.

Gut twisting, Keeva took a deep breath. The woman's voice was ancient and keen, and she knew she dared not lie. "He…he was a friend to me when I had none."

The answer softened the hardness in the sídhe's stare and the woman even smiled a little.

"That's our Idris," the maiden fixing her hair said proudly. "Fairest one, Fairest son, All together, Under one."

The prophetic chant sent an unexpected thrill down Keeva's spine. So. They still believed it, they still believed in their ruined, beautiful prince. How Adoh would hate to know that.

But thinking that cursed one's name seemed dangerous here, and so she buried the thought even as she buried her fists into the folds of her dress and waited for the faeries to finish. They wove delicate vines of silver into her dark hair and strung beads of bright water from her ears. When she dared look into the mirror again, she barely recognized herself without her comfortable furs and leathers. But it wasn't…it wasn't a bad appearance, actually quite pleasing, and she hoped that she wouldn't be such a glaring error in the faerie crowd after all.

"Come, come," the fey women said, tugging her hands and giggling. "Wait until they see what we have done with you!"

All except Idris of course, who couldn't see anything at all. Keeva discovered a vague disappointment in her chest at the thought. Fah. It didn't matter.

She was led out to an enormous glade encircled by the woods, and a garden of fair folk danced upon the lush grass floor. All kinds of musicians, both fey and animal, sat in the surrounding branches and played their wild tunes, which somehow all fit together no matter their variety.

She realized then that she'd been left quite alone, her attendants having flown into the festivities, and so she hung on the edge, twisting her hands uncomfortably. So this was what the Seelie Court looked like. As reputations went, this certainly exceeded it for fairness. Lovely beyond all words. So much so that she felt out of place even in her borrowed finery. She had little wonder then why Idris had been shy to return in his state of imperfection.

Even as she thought of him, he appeared. There, upon the top of a stairway that descended from the trees to the floor of the dancing glade.

The pipes, the fifes, the harps, and lutes, the insects, the leaves, and all the merry folk—went silent.

He wore a robe of autumn colors, deeply hued by the night and changing tones by cast of the light or shadow. Beneath the robe he wore a coat of glittering silver and gold, but even its fine threads could not compare with the shining of his own pale hair. A silken scarf, of the same red as his robe, bound across his eyes and draped far down his back. An ornamental branch of gold curved up from where it clasped behind his slender ear.

But far fairer than his fine feathers was his grace of presence and the change that rippled through the room at the sight of him.

Keeva swallowed hard. She hadn't really realized until this moment just what a royal he was. How fey and above her. She was in no way worthy to be his assassin, and much less to be his chosen guest. This was madness, all of it, and she hated Adoh for having the same powerful effect on her, only one of dread and fear and demanding obedience.

The Seelie prince stepped into the gala, heading somewhere to the glowing arch of whitethorn tress where the king presided over the party. The trill of little winged things began first and then all the other musicians flew back into song with rekindled vigor. The laughter and bells and tapping of feet sprang back into life and all the glade became a flurry of colors.

She took a shy step forward, thinking perhaps to find him or the goblins, but the milling throng before her was an intimidation not to be taken lightly. She began to weave through, attempting to attract as little notice as possible, but more than a few folk glanced her way. Some merely looked, some looked with friendliness, and others…others looked with distaste. She tried to keep her eyes on the ground, but she noticed each and every frown, arch of an eyebrow, and whisper behind a feathered fan.

She couldn't make it. She couldn't go through an entire gauntlet of fey folk to appear before a prince she did not deserve.

Edging back out of the faerie glow, she nearly stumbled over a man with a mushroom hat, or perhaps a mushroom head. He grunted at her with a large brow raised in question of her presence, then stumped towards the gala.

She didn't belong here. She didn't belong anywhere. She was a huntress, forced to the chase, doomed to roam forever.

And so she turned and ran.

10

The thickets of the forest welcomed her flight, all too eagerly cutting off the sight, sounds, and smells of the faerie ring. Very little light shed through the boughs, rendering the ground difficult to navigate, but she hadn't stumbled her way through darkness all her life for nothing, and so the roots and ditches would not slow her down.

Yet something caught her foot, and she flew through the air, coming down in a hard thud to the ground. Groaning, she began to pick herself back up when a red glint caught her gaze.

Not two paces away from her, a red apple rested upon the ground.

She looked immediately up into the branches of the tree whose root she tripped on, but it was merely an old maple. There was no orchard tree to be seen anywhere nearby, and this apple was smooth and fresh.

Her mouth went dry, her stomach sank in dread, and frantic fear spiraled through her mind. Where was he? Where was Adoh and how dare he come inside the Seelie Court? What guise or design he had taken, she scarcely knew. All that mattered was that the apple was here and the duty was hers.

Shaking, she reached out and touched it, half surprised it did not burn the flesh off her fingers.

"Keeva?"

She snatched the apple to her, heart thundering. What even…had she turned around without realizing it or had the very wood sent her back the way she'd come? It didn't matter. What mattered was that Idris stood a little ways off, dark against the glow of the party behind him.

"Are you leaving?" he asked, voice sad.

"I…" She blinked hard, trying to find some semblance of calm. She buried the apple into the folds of her dress and was relieved to find a deep pocket to hide it in. "The noise…the crowd. It was just too much. I needed to breathe."

"Can I join you?"

You don't need my permission to breathe, she thought, even though she knew that was not what he meant. *And if you want to breathe, you'd be better off away from me.*

"You feel unwelcome," he said after a moment.

"It's hard to fit in with perfection," she said, a snide smile cutting across her lips.

"Nobody back there is perfect," he replied. "But….I understand. Why do you think I ran away? People were staring at you, were they not?"

"They had a right." She folded her arms. "I don't fit in anywhere. Not among mortals, not among the Seelie, not among the Unseelie."

"There are foul among the Fair," he admitted. "So I must believe there are fair among the Foul."

Her fingers bit into her skin as memories of shadows and teeth and disdainful eyes swirled across her mind. "I don't know about that."

"Well, why not? There's you."

Oh, how wrong he was. How desperately wrong.

"Do you not dance?" he asked, nodding back to where the musicians made magic under the stars.

"No." She hoped she said it gruffly enough to dispel whatever thought was in his head. It didn't work.

"I am out of practice. Perhaps if you let me show you a few steps I can regain my own confidence?"

She frowned, but there was no use in him noticing that. His hand, partly made of flesh, partly fingered in gold, had already taken her own. It was such a gentle grip, so certain and strong. Without meaning to, she stepped forward as he stepped back. His other hand came to rest at her side and he tapped her toe lightly with his own foot in indication for her to retreat as he advanced.

Perhaps to anyone looking, there would have been little grace in their halting, stumbling movements as she struggled to follow unspoken direction. But the music softly and slowly became a part of their rhythm, and the blink of the fireflies flickered in tune with their steps and the beat of their hearts. And then they were floating across the grass of the glade, perhaps by magic, though of what sort, who could say.

And when he slowed at last to a halt, twirling her free of his hand, she found that she was breathless. She, who scaled mountains and chased stags. Surely it could not be exertion, she thought, pressing a hand to the hard flutter in her chest.

He made a small, clearing noise in his throat and then dipped into a bow. When he rose, his finger was tucked underneath the coat, fiddling with something in a hidden pocket. "I had thought to give this to you later tonight, but…no reason to wait, I suppose."

He cast about for her hand, and she gave it him. Something cool and solid was set in her palm, and she rubbed her fingers around it in question, wanting to see how he'd see it without any eyes. But her sense of touch was not that keen, and so curiosity brought it up to her eyes. There was little light, but what light could be found had all gathered to glint in this small sculpture of diamond. It was a bear. A rearing, roaring bear, perfect in detail no matter that it was hardly bigger than her thumb.

Dohmnal.

"I made it so you could remember what you did. What we did. So you could remember…us."

I'd never forget. She cupped the carving in both hands, almost afraid it would shatter before her very eyes. Its value soared high above the gem from which it was crafted, and she would never, ever let it be lost. "I….thank you."

It was the opportune moment. She could feel the weight of the apple in the deep pocket of her dress, and it seemed ready to rip through the fabric if she kept it hidden a moment more. All she needed to do was withdraw it and say, "I have a gift for you as well. You once mentioned you'd never tasted an apple…"

She could not. She would not. Not now. Not ever.

As thoughtlessly as she'd stolen his heart, so had he softly won hers.

She swallowed hard, determining to throw the apple from the highest mountain as soon as she had half a chance. "Thank you," she said again, and tremblingly set her hand on his arm. "Shall we go back and join the others?"

"We shall," he agreed with a wry smirk. "The goblins might lead us all in their cultural Dance of the Quaking Stones, and that is not an event to miss."

11

Adoh would kill her.

As soon as he realized that she had defied him, he would hunt her down and break every bone in her body. She was not sure if there was anywhere she could run where he would not find her, but she aimed to make a run for it anyway.

When the festivities had passed and they had returned to their mountains as the sun began to rise, she had gone straight to her room with the excuse of needing to sleep away her exhaustion, but in reality, she did nothing of the sort. She set at once to preparing for her flight ahead. The goblins were gone from the house and Idris had retreated to his library, so no one disturbed her when she remerged from the room and crept to the door. A wildcat near the door lifted its head and blinked at her, but made no sound, so she slid the door open and slipped out.

And then she was running, running as fast and as far as her feet would take her. Already, her heart pounded in her chest for fear that Adoh would appear at any moment and demand an explanation.

Despite her best effort, there was a sharp thorn in her heart that hurt with every thud of fear. Idris would not understand. She had not even left him a note. There was nothing he could take from her sudden departure except insult. But it didn't matter, she shouted to herself. It didn't matter what he thought of her, the important part was that she be far away from him! Far away, so he would never know the truth of how dreadfully close she had come to betraying him even after all his kindness. If he knew the truth he would hate her even more, so it was better this way.

On and on she ran through the woods, sometimes slowing when the terrain became too treacherous or when her breath came too fast, but her course was clear. When she reached the nearest human village, she would buy a horse with the savings from her fur sales, and then she would flee from the country. Find somewhere that not even Adoh would dare follow her. A human city perhaps in those lands rumored to be dry and hot, as unlike these lands as could be. It would be a hard change, little more than a cage for her wild and windy spirit, but alive in a cage was better than dead in the cold.

She skidded to a halt at a cliff's edge for just a moment and reached into the satchel at her side. Hands shaking, she withdrew the apple and threw it as far away as possible. The strength in her arm was considerable, and the small red orb faded into a little speck that vanished into the wood.

She exhaled, pressing one hand to her chest to steady her heartbeat. It was done. Idris was safe.

That was when Idris spoke inside her head. "Keeva?"

Idris stood still at the door where his guest stayed and listened for any sound of her stirring. "Keeva?" he said again, but she did not answer. So though he regretted doing so, he pushed the door open and padded to her bed, patting the mattress carefully so as not to put his hand wrong. "Keeva, I am sorry to wake you, but—" He frowned and extended his hand further. She wasn't there. Now that he focused, he could not pick up her presence anywhere nearby.

Leaving the room, he paced out to the main chamber where she often stayed. One of his cats rubbed against his leg, purring, and he reached down to tickle its ears. "Do you know where she went off to?" he murmured.

He heard then the scrape of his front door opening and the cat quickly made a retreat. He tensed. "Keeva, is that you?"

"Sorry, Idris." Her fair voice sounded mildly abashed and her footsteps shy and soft.

"Weren't you sleeping?"

"Couldn't. Last night was too thrilling."

He smiled slightly, fiddling with the end of his scarf. "I'm glad. I know you feared going, so I wanted to thank you again for coming."

"No, Idris, it's—" She paused, never sounding more hesitant. "It is I who must thank you. So I went and found you a gift."

"You shouldn't have," he said, stepping back in surprise. "What is it?"

He could hear her hand rustle in her coat and withdraw something smooth and small. "An apple," she said.

"NO!" Keeva screamed hopelessly to the open sky, startling birds from the trees. "No, no, NO! Idris, stop it, stop it, it isn't me! Idris!!!" Somehow, *somehow*, she thought her voice should reach him. Never mind the distance, never mind her lack of any magical skill, he *had* to hear her.

She could only hear his side of the conversation, but she could guess all too well who served in her stead at the other end.

Turning so hard that the ground tore beneath her boot, she sped back the way she came. But there was no way, no possible way she could arrive in time. She could only run and listen to him speak to her. Speak what could only be his final words.

"I understand you've never tasted one."

He rubbed the apple in his fingers, feeling how slick and firm it was. The aroma of it was certainly compelling. "I haven't," he said.

"Then please, try a single bite."

He hesitated as he reached up to unwrap the sash from his head. For a moment he had to remember that his bare face had already been seen, that he could not keep up the habit of hiding it in shame. So with a hard swallow, he let the cloth down and raised the apple to his lips.

He paused. "Keeva," he said, pouring every bit of summer warmth into the word. "I trust you." His teeth bit into the apple's crisp flesh with a crunch.

I trust you.

The silence that followed in Keeva's ears was akin to the dead.

12

Keeva huddled alone on the snowy floor of the woods, rocking back and forth, trying to hold in the sobs that were swelling within her. She clutched the small carving of Dohmnal in her hand, palm and fingers pressing hard enough to hurt.

He was gone and who knew where Adoh had taken him or even if he was still alive. He spoke to her no more, no matter how many times she keened his name.

Something softly stirred nearby, and she lifted her tear-stained face to see that she had attracted a small audience. A few birds flocked in the encircling trees, cocking their heads at her, and in the brush below, the beady eyes of a weasel peered out. A few rabbits wiggled their noses at her from behind a clump of grass.

She stared dumbly at them a moment as more and more animals appeared. Idris's pets... Her cries had not gone entirely unheard. They knew his name. Indeed, she doubted that there was not a creature on the mountain who didn't know him.

"Please," she whispered. "Can you help me? For his sake?" The words sounded so foolish the moment they slipped from her mouth that she bit her tongue immediately after.

But then something much larger stepped out of the shadow of the wood and she found herself staring up into at the magnificent visage of a stag. He was an ancient, beautiful creature, and she could not help but think of the one that she'd nearly shot before meeting Idris. It lowered its mighty head and sniffed her in a deep huff, and she sat perfectly petrified. Its dark soft eye met hers and there was an intelligence in the depths of that gaze which she could not fathom.

"Do you understand me?" she murmured. "Would you take me back to the goblins? They must know what has happened." She rose slowly to her feet, and though the stag tossed its rack it did not bolt. Tentatively, she reached out to its withers and brushed her hand down its hide. Then, before she could change her mind, before she could convince herself such an idea was stupidity, she flung herself up onto the stag's back. It pranced in place, and she nearly slid off. But it was letting her; it was actually willing to help. "Take me back! They may know the only way to reach the King. He's the only one who can help Idris."

With a deep whistling bellow, the stag plunged forward, and all the little animals darted about its hooves in an effort to keep up. She clung with all her might around its neck, legs pressed tight into its sides in an effort to stay on. It was nothing like riding a horse, far more wild and graceful at once.

It plunged back up the mountain slope, closing the distance she had ventured in half the time it had taken her to make it. Even so, it felt far too long before the top of the mountain and the doorway to Idris's home came in sight.

All seven goblins were already gathered on the slope outside, grunting and growling, and they were not the only ones. She recognized the Seelie King and his Loresman even at a distance, and her heart plummeted. If only they would give her a chance to explain before killing her…

The goblins saw her coming first and pointed in great excitement. She supposed she made quite an entrance surrounded by the woodland creatures and hoped they earned her a chance to speak.

The stag slowed alongside the king, and he looked up at Keeva with both distrust and hope. "Where is my son?"

"Your Majesty," she swallowed hard, not yet willing to dismount from the stag. "I believe Adoh has broken the locks of his life and taken him away from here."

"I know, I felt it," he said angrily, and she flinched at the heat in his eyes. He reached up and dragged her off the stag with one sweep of his arm. She completely lost all height advantage and had to crane her neck to look at him. "What I want to know is how *you* know of Adoh and the enchantment."

"D-don't kill me," she stammered, looking to the goblins for help. They looked worried for her, but also suspicious. She'd be on her own. She stiffened her spine and met the king's gaze square on. "I am Adoh's changeling child. I have obeyed his commands all my life until now. Your son was kind to me, and I could not betray him in the end. I ran. But it seems that Adoh has broken the last lock on his own."

The goblins murmured, whether in anger or disappointment, she could hardly tell. Probably both. As for the king, she could not read his gaze. "I have come back to help if I can," she said. "Do you think I would have come here, knowing you could kill me, if I did not want to reverse my sin? Idris cannot die because of me. We have to find him as soon as possible."

The Loresman stepped to the king's side, tilting his head and narrowing his intense eyes at her. "She speaks with sincerity, Deorsa."

"I know," the king growled. He let her go with a snap of his hand, and she stumbled back. "Do you know where he is? The Loresman and I have already looked for him, but his spirit is hidden from us, shrouded in shadow. If you are familiar with Adoh's realm, where would you suggest we look?"

She reeled for an answer, thinking of an endless number of places. There was every matter of dark prison in the Unseelie Court…it was too vast an expanse to search.

When she failed to answer in anything beyond a stammer, he spoke again. "Answer this, mortal. How did Adoh learn of the correct keys to break the enchantment?"

"I don't know." She clenched her teeth. "He only told me what they were, not how he got them."

The king paced back and forth, a lion savage for a kill. "Only the Loresman and I knew what locked the enchantment!" He paused then, and the anger upon his face flared then refocused into something sharp and deadly. He wheeled upon the Loresman.

The fey had already fallen to his knees, hands up to stall his sovereign's wrath. "My King!" he cried. "I have not betrayed you! But…" His throat bobbed, and misery was in his eyes. "But I have failed you. There….there was one other who knew of the enchantment's secrets."

"How is this possible if not by betrayal?" Deorsa growled in a low rumble of thunder.

The Loresman looked so sick Keeva almost would have felt sorry for him if she wasn't waiting for the answer with the same angry expectation.

"It is not I who created the enchantment," the Loresman whispered. "When you asked for it, I studied and searched, but there was nothing I could create on my own to prevent death. So I went looking for another more powerful…I went to Loch Mor."

Deorsa paled.

"What does that mean?" Keeva demanded. In all her time in the dark court and under Adoh's tutelage, she'd never heard the name.

"Loch Mor, the realm of Fuath…….Lord of the Dead."

⚜

Night forever hung over Loch Mor. Its thick waters reflected black, and even if stars did sometimes dare to peep from behind the brooding clouds, their light never once winked upon the surface of the lake.

The shrubbery on the shore of the loch suddenly moved with a rapid wind, and the air cut open. A pale figure in white was thrown through the tear, and after it stepped a dark figure. The portal closed immediately afterwards.

The eerie amity of the loch's eternal night was broken by the cackling laughter of Adoh. He loomed above the body of the fallen prince, throwing his head back to the sky in unbound glee. "So simple! So simple a plan, so simple a fool!" He kicked Idris hard.

The prince rolled away and rose up onto his hands and knees, spitting the remnants of the apple from his mouth.

"It's too late," Adoh sneered. "It's already been done. You feel it, do you not? The precious locks on your life are undone, and you are just as vulnerable as the rest of us!"

"I feel it, Adoh," he said bitterly. "It would seem you'll finally have your way." He slowly rose up, leaning back onto his heels. "I am almost surprised you persisted this long. But it was low, even for you, to bring Keeva into it."

"Keeva." Adoh chuckled, pacing back and forth before him. "Ah yes, Keeva. You think her an innocent bystander in this, don't you? You think I merely took her guise to trick you?"

The prince said nothing.

"No, no, no." Adoh paused for a moment, swooping so low to him that Idris veered slightly back. "In fact, Keeva has been mine all along. She was the one who unlocked your first protections! She came up that mountain hunting for you, not that bear! Fah, she was mine from the start!"

And still the prince said nothing, but Adoh was lost in the revel of his triumph and railed on.

"You naïve boy! Even after me, you learned nothing. I thought the girl might win your friendship, but she took something else from you, didn't she? So then, how does it feel to have your heart broken?"

Idris laughed.

The world surrounding them exhaled. Even the wind stopped stirring the trees, even the water stilled. Adoh paused mid-step and slowly turned to face his enemy. An enemy who, in his greatest moment of peril, was laughing.

Idris raised his chin, the shadow of his laugh still cast across the air. "Do not take me for a fool, Adoh," he said. "I knew she served you from the moment I felt iron on my brow."

For a long awful moment, Adoh stared. A sharp hiss inhaled between his clenched teeth. "You lie. Why….would you have not killed her? Sent her away? If you knew she meant to betray you, why pretend otherwise?"

"Because when she spoke of the Unseelie man who stole her as a baby, she spoke with fear," Idris replied. "She was trapped, and I pity any who suffer under your hand. So I wanted her to know instead what trust felt like. Friendship. Loyalty."

"Ha," Adoh said softly, then again in a loud bark. "You and your childish fancies of mercy. You failed!"

Idris smiled at him, and it was a far more terrible smile than anything the Unseelie King could conjure. "Did I? Then how come it was you who brought me the apple?"

Adoh roared, sounding more like a wild bear in that moment than any faerie. "Insolent cur! I will be done with you once and for all!" He sprang upon the prince and caught him fast by the hair at the nape of his neck, jerking his head back to expose his naked neck.

"Before you kill me," Idris said, wincing at the strain of his neck from Adoh's grip. "Tell me why. Why have you hated me so?"

Adoh spat a hard laugh. "You ask! Should I not take such a prophecy as a threat to my throne, even if it speaks of a whelp like you? But no…you are right, my hatred runs deeper still. How is it that such a prophecy be spoken of you when it should have been spoken of my son? On this day, when you are dead at last, it is my son who should rise and claim the throne! It was always he who was the more deserving!"

"But Adoh…" Idris said softly. "You don't have a son."

Silence.

Silence as deep and dark as the waters in the loch.

"He died," Idris continued. "As an infant, in the same plague that took my mother. My father sent you a tribute of grief, but you never replied."

After a moment sodden in grieving understanding, he spoke again, but this time with an edge of suspicion and anger. "To take a human child requires leaving another in its place. Did you exchange your dead son for Keeva? Did you hope somehow she would replace him? And when she couldn't, was that when you decided she should be nothing more than a tool for your revenge?"

"If taking your tongue did not silence you," Adoh said, teeth grinding together. "Then I will just have to take your head." He tightened his fingers in the prince's hair and yanked back harder, pressing the iron knife to his throat.

"Adoh," Fuath said.

Both fey men startled at the voice.

Adoh had forgotten that the loch was not so empty and lonely a witness as the silence had suggested. The waters rippled with an eerie glow, and the face of Fuath flickered upon the surface, somehow almost seeming to rise upwards.

Idris, though unable to see the creature, pulled back hard against his captor's grip and frowned at the uninvited presence.

"Adoh, our exchange for the knowledge of the three keys is not yet complete. I have yet to name my price.""Name it then!" the Unseelie King barked. "Idris," the monster in the loch said. "I claim Idris."

13

Adoh stared at the monster in the loch for a long moment, the knife in his hand quivering. "You can have him," he said at last. "As soon as I slit his throat, I will toss his corpse into your waters."

"No," Fuath said, smiling as smooth and slick as the green film upon his surface. "I'm afraid I need him before he is dead."

His teeth bared in a feral scowl, Adoh dragged Idris back from the water. "What treachery is this, Fuath? Have I not bargained with you for years so that I could accomplish this?"

"The Loresman bargained to protect this prince's life; you bargained to take it. But you hardly cared to know the price anymore after the second attempt. The price is Idris. Give him to me."

"Never." Froth dripped over Adoh's lips. "You lying wretch...his life is mine to take."

A horn rang through the bitter cold air. A golden horn of pure light, joined by another, and then another, until the sound was so bright the night was almost forgotten.

As Adoh stared in slack horror, Idris moved. He twisted in the Unseelie King's grip, jabbing an elbow back into his side, and broke free. The Unseelie reached after him, claws extended, but as he did, something hissed through the air. Adoh screamed and recoiled, an arrow pierced through his hand.

A mighty host broke through the dark forest, bringing the colors of the season with them. All manner of fair folk, armed to the teeth, and at their head was the Seelie King, a troop of snarling goblins, and a stag upon which rode…

Adoh hissed as he met eyes with Keeva, and he snapped her arrow with savage force. But the sight of her had distracted him from his first and more important vengeance, and when he looked for Idris again, he saw that the prince had already reached his people. No. No. NO. Victory would not be stolen from him; he could not come this close and fail! He threw back his head and shrieked and the sound carried to all corners of his realm. For if Deorsa brought his armies here for a reckoning, a reckoning he would have….

"Idris," Keeva gasped as he finished assuring his father of his safety. He turned to her, hand searching for something to touch, and he found the head of the stag. He smiled in surprise and scratched its jaw as it nuzzled into his shoulder, and then reached with his other hand for her.

"I knew you would come," he said, his smirk far too light and airy for one who'd skirted death.

She stared at him dumbly. "What do you mean, you knew?"

"Well, you got my message didn't you?"

"But you were…you were….are you saying, you knew Adoh wasn't m—"

A cry rose up from the fair folk. In the forest, further away from them, a great many things were moving, and as they watched, all kinds of ugly creatures spilled from the dark roots and boughs. They gathered at Adoh's back, slavering and scraping at the ground.

Keeva's heart sank. The Unseelie Court had come, and they'd come in droves. Adoh would have war.

"They would seek mastery over us," the Unseelie King cried to his armies. "Tonight, take our fate back into our hands!" The court stirred at his words, shaking their weapons and growling in a rising swell.

The Seelie folk tensed in response, looking to their king. Deorsa scowled at his enemy, but before he could utter a command, the dark court of foul folk surged forward with the anger of their ruler at their backs. In response, the Seelie shouted and brandished their weapons. The goblins growled and hefted huge hammers of stone. Keeva leapt from her stag and knelt on the steady ground as she strung an arrow to her bow and waited for a clear shot.

Upon the shore of Loch Mor, the fey rushed one another, the vision of blood already spilling from their eyes.

"ENOUGH!"

The word shouted in every mind, loud enough to send many cringing. They could not have escaped the voice had their ears been stuffed with cotton or if they'd been miles away. It spoke within them and reverberated to the core.

Idris strode between the two armies, his arms held out, and his voice called forth again, "Enough of this! Why do you fight, Unseelie? Because your king summoned you here? Do you know why? *Someone* tell me why!"

"Slay him!" Adoh thrust his arm out like a javelin. "Strike him down before he utters another word."

"They will not," Idris said calmly. Indeed, the throng of wild creatures and dark monsters had halted and they glanced back and forth from the terrible and glorious Seelie Court to their own furious king. Then their gazes returned to rest upon the snow white prince, and there they remained entranced. "You see, Adoh, not all of them hate me as you do. I believe there are many who have longed for peace and goodwill between the Day and the Night. They welcomed me in your court so long ago. But did they know what you did?" He whirled to face the forces of the dark folk. "Do you?"

And he illuminated himself in light so that they could look upon the ruin their king had wrought. A wave of stunned sorrow rippled through the mass, and many of them whimpered or winced at the harsh sight of what they'd heard only through whispers and jeers.

Keeva had never seen such a display of regret from the Unseelie folk, and she marveled that they had loved and wanted this being of light to bring them a hope they hardly knew.

"You fight tonight," Idris said, "at the bitterness and hatred of another man. I want only for the animosity among our peoples to end. No more blood. Not tonight." He reached up and touched his face, uttering a small growl. "What was done to me is done. I do not know if it is still possible to fulfill the prophecy as so many of you had hoped. But I would try, even so."

"No!" Adoh screamed. "You will die!" Even as he lunged forward, blade raised for the kill, Idris stepped deftly out of reach.

But the step took the prince to the edge of the loch—and the waters moved.

Fuath rose from the lake.

As flat and wavering as his reflection, he seized hold of Idris by the shoulders. And then he pulled him straight back to fall into the loch with a sharp slap. The water rippled once and then stilled.

Keeva screamed and she was the first to reach the lake's edge. Without a thought, she plunged in and waded out to Idris's body which lay strangely placid under the surface. She reached in to seize him and…her blood ran cold, far colder than even the chill of the dark loch. She could not touch him. She could not feel him. It was like he wasn't even there. Yet there he floated, as still and serene as a corpse in a coffin and the lake surface as a glass lid. Even his hands were folded over his chest. Only his hair moved in the water's pulse. She thrashed at the water, trying her hardest to reach him or even disturb the image. But it was no use. No matter what she saw, he was not there.

Deorsa had taken only one horrified step forward before he froze. Because without looking, he knew. He felt it. The bright warm sense that always rested against his heart flickered and went dull. Gone. His beautiful, beloved son was gone.

The eyes of the Seelie King snapped to Adoh.

Adoh stood as one transfixed, a cruel satisfied smile jarring his teeth. The satisfaction was a bitter one, a dream realized in an undesired way, but achieved nonetheless. He knew the moment Deorsa looked at him, and his smile bared wider.

The ground rippled beneath Adoh's feet, and his smile slipped. Gripping the hilt of his sword, he edged back along the tree-line, hooded eyes snapping with dark lighting. Deorsa circled opposite him, and death stared out from his gaze.

14

Idris opened his eyes.

It took him a few moments of staring at the wavering dark waters around him to remember he shouldn't be seeing anything at all. He gasped and then choked, immediately expecting his lungs to be filled with liquid. He discovered then the second impossibility. He wasn't wet, and he knelt on something solid….not quite ground, but solid despite its slippery gloss.

As he stared down in disbelief at the strange floor, he saw that the hands braced in front of his face were healed and perfectly whole. "No," he whispered. "No…." Confusion turned to panic, and he surged up to his feet, reeling backwards to catch his balance.

He stood in a throne room unlike any other. Its pillars and walls were clear as glass, yet utterly dark for whatever lay beyond. Something about them was not right; they moved as if made of jelly. A putrid order filled the hall, a stench of decay and mud. As he slowly turned in observation, he came to face the master of the realm.

Upon a throne of bones and slime, Fuath sat. He was little more than that himself, an enormous skeleton upon which clung rotting flesh and algae. His eyes were like that of a sea serpent, green and bulbous. The weeds of the loch robed him and a rack of horns was upon his skull. He dripped with darkly stained water.

Idris scowled at the sight of him, little questioning whose presence he stood in. His hand flew to his belt and he withdrew a knife, something he rarely ever relied on, but felt better with now. "What have you done?" he demanded, gagging over the feel of using his own tongue again. "What kind of glamour is this?"

Fuath waved a careless hand at the knife. "Do not bother yourself with that, dear one, I am already dead. As for you, you should be thanking me. It is because of me that you are still alive."

"It is because of you that I am here," Idris snarled. "I owe you no thanks."

It was strange for a skull to yet bear expression, but Fuath's visage twisted in amusement nonetheless. "Ah, you owe me far more thanks than you realize, prince. It was I who gave the Loresman the enchantment to protect you to begin with."

"Which you gave Adoh the keys to in some kind of deal. A deal to acquire me," Idris said quickly.

"You see clearly for a man who was blind."

Idris's hand tightened on his knife, not caring that the weapon was useless. "Perhaps blindness improved my listening. So explain, Fuath. Why would you pit us against each other? Why would you want me alive?"

For a long moment, Fuath did not answer. He only tapped his bony finger upon his throne arm, letting that sound linger in a tick-tock around them. "I hear of little in these wretched halls save what whispers are left on dying lips. But I have heard of your prophecy. A prophecy of hope. A prophecy where you rule the fair and the foul and there is peace. A prophecy….you are no longer able to fulfill. Unless—"

At the final tap of his finger, the wall beside Idris swelled and moved forward. He jerked to face it, startled at the figure within, but then he paused. For he looked upon his own reflection. The reflection of the prince he once had been, the prince he seemed to be now.

"What would you say," Fuath purred, "if I could give you back what was lost."

The knife shook in Idris's hand. "This is a lie," he said. "You're lying."

"Am I? You doubt my power. I withheld death itself for you. You would be a fool to not at least consider the possibility. Do you really want to bear the shame of *this* face forever? Do you want *this* to be what others look upon?"

As he spoke, the reflection in the mirror changed. Idris could still see it, and he looked for the first time upon his own ruin. His breath sucked in sharp and short, and his fists clenched. It…it was difficult to look upon, made worse by the perfection that had stared at him a second ago. The scars of his missing eyes were so strange and unnerving, and his hands so clumsy and awkward.

"It's still me," he whispered, but his voice shook. "The people who love me know that."

"The people who love you. As if that were *all* that mattered. There are two kingdoms depending upon you, upon that fair face, upon the prophecy! It would only require a very simple price."

"A price of what?" Idris growled, his hand slowly falling to his side as he stared at his long-lost face.

"Three drops of blood. No more."

Idris wheeled on him. "My *blood?* You would seek to control me! You are nothing but a carrion scavenger! You deceived the Loresman! You manipulated Adoh in his grief! I will *never* enter into a deal with you!"

Fuath rose from his throne, stained water gushing from his robes and his teeth bared in a predatory gleam.

Something changed.

Something tore and shifted in the fabric of the worlds.

Idris fell to his knees as a weight descended upon him. For one moment, he thought it was the power of Adoh. But it was something else. Something far greater, far more terrible. His blood rushed with energy unlike any other, and he felt the confines of his spirit stretch and expand in a painful thrill.

He felt the power of his own kingship.

His only thought was one broken word.

Father…

⚶

"Loresman!" Keeva shouted, racing to the faerie's side. "Is there any way we can go in after Idris?"

"Impossible," the Loresman said, tearing his gaze away from the forest where the two kings battled in a fury of sparks and bracken. "Fuath's enchantments are strong, and I cannot break through the locks on his doors."

"But what about the door that has no lock?" She held her knife tight in her hand, although none of the Unseelie Court had moved forward to attack. "I am a mortal. If Fuath thinks like the Unseelie Court, he will leave openings for mortals to stumble into. He is a predator, and he hungers. Mortals such as I are prey, and not a threat. Send me through. I'll help Idris as I can."

He looked at her in surprise, brow furrowing. "It might work…he may let you pass."

"Send me." She turned away from the sounds of chaos and raced back to the lake. She could already feel the Loresman's magic racing after her, propelling her speed. And when she dove into the water beside Idris's body, she felt the change. The press of resistance, the tearing of seams, and then—she was through.

She opened her eyes and found herself in the halls of the Loch Mor.

∽∾

The air bristled with the smell and sound of burning needles, crackling and disintegrating from inner embers.

"What did you want, Adoh?" Deorsa demanded as he advanced. "Is all this because you wanted me to know the pain of losing my son? Did you want me to feel the ache of knowing all my hopes for him were stolen to the east wind? Did you want me to understand the burning, consuming need for revenge? DID YOU?" The next sweep of his hand brought the roots bursting from the ground and knocked Adoh from his feet. The Seelie King loomed above him, robes swelling in the shift of heat and cold. "If that was indeed your intent," Deorsa whispered, blade gleaming as he drew it from the scabbard, "then you succeeded."

Adoh scrambled back to a stand, but the earth beneath his feet could no longer be trusted and the trees themselves were the enemy, reaching out with clawing branches, glittering eyes glaring from between the boughs. A crazed laugh spilled from Adoh's lips, and he flung a snarl of scorn at the avenger. "You cannot kill me! It is written in the Law that no King may take the other King's life with his own hand! Is it not so, Deorsa? You would not disobey the Law!"   The Seelie King reached up to the crown atop his own head and cast it to the ground. Adoh stared as one condemned at the crown as it rolled through the mud and vanished under a tangle of brambles. The sickened smile was still frozen on his lips in that moment that Deorsa's sword cleft his head from his shoulders. The two crowns lay lost in the darkening shadows and the pooling of blood.

15

The slippery, ever moving walls of Loch Mor sent a shudder through Keeva, and then she was creeping across the wet ground, following a pale green light that cast through the shadowed corridors. This faerie realm stank of more horror than even the Unseelie Court, but she refused to consider that. First Idris. Then they could fight whatever came their way together.

She heard muted voices and hurried in pursuit. As she turned a corner, she beheld them. The lord of the loch and the sídhe prince she held dear. Fuath was awful to the eye, but she did not waste a glance on him, instead looking to Idris. An Idris she hardly recognized. He was whole and he was beautiful, and she staggered to a stop in dismay.

He was upon his knees, his head cradled in his hands.

"You feel it." The monster sneered. "Your father is slain. The crown and the power are yours. Swear yourself to me, and all that you once were I will give back to you. You cannot fulfill the prophecy without your beauty. I can give it back."

"I will never serve you," Idris spat.

As she watched, Fuath lifted his dripping arm. "Willing or not, you will serve my purpose. The prophecy cannot be fulfilled if you are here in my realm. The wars which will rage above shall profit many dead, and my halls shall be filled to bursting. Go then to your doom. If you will not accept my gift, go and sleep and dream in the dark." His arm flung out, caught Idris in the chest, and threw him through the watery walls.

Keeva shouted as the loch swallowed Idris in a slurping gulp, and she charged forward across the hall as Fuath turned to her. He relaxed back against his throne of rotting bones, and waved a hand in the way Idris had vanished.

"So you have pursued him this far, mortal creature? Reckless are you to enter here, but mortals do seek death so often. Continue in your hunt then, I will not stop you."

She wished for nothing more than to leap up the steps and sink her knife between his ribs, but she knew already that would accomplish nothing. So with a savage snarl, she did just as he said. She plunged through the wall after the prince.

It was the most awful feeling, far worse than even entering the loch. The jellied wall sucked at her skin as if it wished to pull it from her body and she felt as if she sunk downwards. But at the end of the sink, she did not hit ground, but broke free into the open. The loch outside of the halls spread out before her, dark and fathomless. It wavered in front of her eyes and was thick to move though, as if it were still water, but she could breathe despite the panic seizing her heart.

He could be anywhere. He could be in places she'd never reach. Who was she to think that she could find him?

She was his huntress. She would find him if it…if it killed her, and if it did, then her spirit would wander these waters forever in the seeking.

Deeper and deeper she plunged into the loch, and she called his name often. Nothing alive could be seen down here, no fish, no growing plant, just drifting weeds and glowing green souls floating sadly by.

Then something changed. She began to notice that some of the green lights were blinking at her in the dark, and when she turned to look at them, they vanished entirely. A chill crawled up the nape of her neck, resting in a tickle at the edge of her ears. Those were not lost little souls…those were eyes.

She stilled, hunkered as far into herself as she could go. Every sort of unwanted memory squirmed their way to the surface of her thought. Memories of her childhood. For every child is afraid of eyes in the dark, but for her, those eyes had been real. She had no one to come in with a light and banish the monsters away, for she lived with the monsters and she was one of them. A changling child. A pawn of the Unseelie Court.

"Go away," she whispered, as the scene around her shifted. "Go away, go away, go away." But it was coming to her, brought in vivid clarity. The thick black forests with their sharp and pointing branches. The bogs in which lurked things with long sticky fingers that reached out for ankles. The eyes became more numerous, winking in mirth at her fear. With a savage cry, she pulled up her bow and strung an arrow. "Stay back, you miserable beasts!"

When she'd finally grown, surviving the court and all its terrors, she'd convinced Adoh to release her to her own kind. To learn of their ways so that she might blend in and be better suited to his use. How terrifying it had been to enter the human lands, but how much better to leave the land of terror behind. And she was not going back, not now, not here, not ever!

Wrenching away from the gathering eyes, she fled. She fled through the forests and their poking branches, she fled through the bog and leapt clear of the reaching hands. Forgetting Idris in a moment of terror, she raced to be free of the surrounding haunt.

Without warning, she ran straight into the open door of the Unseelie Court. She gasped and turned back to go the way she'd come, but whatever door she'd passed through was gone now. So she crouched down in the dark and trembled. It was so pitch black she could not even see her own hand when she held it in front of her face.

This is how it would end. She would be trapped forever in her own nightmare.

Now that the feast is over and the guests have gone, there is a matter I wish to discuss—a private matter, if you please.

She started at the sound of Adoh's voice, far away. Bile rose in her throat and she began to clamp her hands over her ears when she heard another voice answer. A voice she knew and loved.

"Idris?" she whispered. Struggling up on her weakened legs, she followed the sound of the distant voices.

Please, you are not thinking, you will dishonor your people forever.

The distress in Idris's voice quickened her steps, but they were yet so far away and she could still see nothing. But already, an uncomfortable suspicion was rising in her mind, and the moment she heard the scream of pain, she knew it was true.

She was not trapped in her nightmare.

She was trapped in his.

The scream drew her in a race to its end, and she willed the sound of her own feet and heaving breath to drown out the cries of pain from the prince. This couldn't be happening to him again, not even in a dream. She had to stop it.

And at last they appeared before her. Not the court, just the figures in the dark. None of them seemed to see her as she shoved through them for they were too intent in their glee towards the white figure huddled on the ground in their midst. A figure whose beautiful golden hair was now dark with ink and whose fair skin was now stained in red.

The horror of the sight stumbled her to a stop, and she stood among the jeering crowd, gaping at the ruin of the faerie prince. It shouldn't have been this way. He hadn't deserved it.

Why and how could anyone, even Adoh, be so cruel? But he was not the only cruel one. She stared around at the surrounding folk and she thought that there were many more of them than had been in the real event. In reality, she had heard it was only Adoh and his greatest lords, but here many of the Unseelie folk watched and guffawed and worse still she thought she saw some of the Seelie folk observing without pity.

She was one of them. The knowledge descended upon her as if a great stone had been strung about her neck. She choked, falling to the ground. Here, she judged these monsters for harming him, but how was she any different? Had she not gone to deceive him, to strip him of the protections upon his life? She had hurt him, first by stealing his breath, and then by prick of iron. Small but vital steps to his destruction.

Still on her hands and knees, she crawled through the nightmare till she was by his side. Her hand clutched his bloody one and she bent her head to his. "I'm sorry," she whispered. "I'm sorry for what I have done, Idris. I am a monster like the rest of them, but I am sorry." Her tears splashed down upon his fingers.

His head tilted and turned to her. She gasped, for she had thought him no more than a vision same as the rest of those who cavorted about them, but as his hand tightened around hers, she knew without a shadow of a doubt that this was the real Idris.

Impossibly, he smiled. "I know," he said softly. "I've known for some time. I forgave you long ago."

She gaped at him, not sure whether to feel hope, confusion, or anger. Possibly all of them at once. "Why didn't you say so?! Why did you play along with my deception instead of confronting me?"

"I wanted *you* to tell me. I wanted you to make your own decision." He brushed his mangled hand up her cheek, melting her rigid stance, and his lips brushed her cheek. "I only ever wanted you to be free."

At the touch of his kiss, the visions around them blurred and swept apart. They were alone in the dark but they could see each other, and the blood and fresh wounds were gone, leaving him behind as he was…still scarred, but the Idris she knew and loved.

"Thank you for finding me and pulling me out of that," he said squeezing her hands. "You remind me of my purpose." He took a deep breath and straightened, drawing both of them back up to their feet.

"Fuath!" he shouted, and the ring of his voice cut through the murk of the loch.

Fuath appeared, the lingering flesh on his face twisting into the sourest form possible. Keeva braced at the sight of him, her hand falling to her knife, but Idris had her other arm looped through his and he patted it comfortingly.

"Fuath, you have made an error," Idris said.

"Have I?" the monster of the loch snarled.

"Indeed you have. As you yourself stated, I am now King of the Courts and so its power is mine. And you are the Lord of the Dead. Fuath....I am not *dead*."

With those words, the world around them began to swell and move with water, not stagnant water, but living and rushing. The darkness faded back as more and more of the loch came forward. Vines shot up somewhere from the murky floor and spread along the invisible walls of the dark realm, piercing and shattering them. From somewhere above, light began to shimmer in starburst brilliance, casting rays of pale gold into the deep.

Fuath wailed and surged forward, but in that moment Idris stepped to the door that his vines had sundered, and they broke from his realm.

The loch was merely a loch in truth again, and the Lord of the Dead could be seen no more. Keeva choked in surprise, bubbles bursting up in front of her vision, and she was overwhelmed by the coldness of the lake. For a moment they floundered there, and then Idris caught her to his side and struck for the surface. They emerged with a splash, choking on what drops of water they had swallowed in the struggle.

Keeva splashed forward and felt her feet touch the silty floor of the loch. She tried once to stand, but fell over, and so instead crawled up onto the bank. She flung herself onto the solid ground and rolled over to stare up at the stars. She was certain she had never really appreciated their lively sparkle until now.

Idris collapsed beside her, heaving for breath. His hand felt about for her and she grasped it in assurance. "You did it," she wheezed. "We're safe now."

"Idris! Idris!"

The goblins were the first to notice them come up from the water, and they rushed to their side, heaving them up and patting them in a harsh but loving inspection of their living existence. Right behind them came the Loresman, face slack with relief, and after him came Deorsa.

When Deorsa touched his son in an effort to get past the goblins for an embrace of his own, Idris drew back as if stung.

"Father?" he said, face wrinkling in confusion. "But…but…I am king…I felt the transfer of power. I thought you had died."

Without an answer, his father caught him close and held him, and Idris relaxed with wonder and joy despite not understanding. But at last, Deorsa leaned back. He smiled as he looked upon his son, stroking his wet hair away from his face. "Yes, you are king," he said. "I gave up the throne so I could kill Adoh."

"Father!"

Somehow, it both surprised and didn't surprise Keeva that there was actual and real regret for Adoh's fate in Idris's tone. He *would* pity him; he just would.

"I do not regret it," his father said stubbornly. "But…" A soft pride glinted in his eyes. "But your compassion is why you are the Fairest. Why you are King of both the Courts."

He stepped aside as he spoke so that behind him could be seen a great gathering.

The courts had watched the battle between the kings and they had watched both crowns strike the ground. They had looked in distress to the body of Adoh and the figure of Deorsa, and they as one had looked to the water where Idris had vanished. Everyone remembered the prophecy's words and waited to see if it would come to pass.

They looked at him now, both the beastly and the beautiful, and their faces were filled with hope and anxiety.

Idris stepped towards them, feeling their thoughts if not seeing, and held out his hand. After a few steps forward, it came to rest on an Unseelie fey, who flinched but did not draw back.

"What is your name?" he asked.

"Tolork, Fairest One."

"Torlork. I once was fairest, but that is now lost. But would you take me for your king?"

The fey eyed him up and down. "If I am honest, I am more comfortable with you now than I ever was before. I feel perhaps you might understand me."

"I will strive to," Idris said honestly. "I will try to be a just and fair ruler to all the people."

"Then yes, I will follow you."

"And so will I," cried another Unseelie.

"So will I!" a Seelie shouted.

"So will I, if you can forgive me for my foolishness," the Loresman said.

"I will follow you as my king," Deorsa said with a smile. "And perhaps learn from your ways."

Keeva dared not speak any words to draw his attention, although she longed to. She could only watch in amazement as both the courts gathered to him. Yet though most rushed forward, there were many from both courts who slunk away and disappeared into the shadows, for they had never wished the prophecy to be fulfilled.

His hand touched her arm and she startled, looking up at him with wide, anxious eyes. She would learn now exactly what his forgiveness meant.

"Be my Queen?" he asked.

She blinked. Her mind stalled. "Is…that the same thing as your bride?"

"That's what I meant, yes," he said, reddening.

She stared at him in consternation, wondering if he even felt any doubt that he should be asking such a ridiculous question. She, a mortal, and one all too recently his enemy. But it didn't matter to him, and suddenly, it didn't matter to her either. So what if she wasn't worthy? He had deemed her so, and the realization of that swelled her heart so full that it hurt. She was forgiven, she was wanted, she was loved, and it felt better than she'd ever dreamed.

"Yes," she said simply and smiled.

The court followed their new King and the huntress upon his arm, and they passed through the forests together in a procession of light and shadow like the glowing of embers. The banshees and sylphs led the way in wild song, all the creatures of the forest gathering to see.

Fairest one, fairest son,

All together, under one,

Kingdoms twain, now together

A crown to last, for now, forever

And even in the villages far away, men stopped their work and listened. For upon the wind, there was a sweet sigh, a sound of spring and promise and the beginning of lives restored.

Finis

Now behold a new court.

The sundered sídhe are together again and they dance in the same glades. Not all of them are fair, but there is loveliness even in the strange and broken. Nowhere is this seen better than in their King and Queen.

For the Queen was once mortal and outcast, but there is pride now in her eye and her hand is strong. A bow is often upon her back as she leads the Court in the Hunt, for there is no one else with an aim more true.

And see now the King robed in forest leaves and summer sun. A great crown of glittering branches sweeps from his brow and along his shining hair, and a scarf of emerald is bound across his scarred face. His smile is kind and the wise hand with which he rules is bright with gold.

For the broken are beautiful when they rise from the shadows and welcome the brightening dawn.

ᔰ Acknowledgements ᔰ

Where would I be without my beloved family? You are the best in the world, giving me joy, encouragement, and love. Thank you for supporting my dreams of writing and for listening to my stories aloud.

A huge thank you to my beta readers: Bryn Shutt, Rebeka Borshevsky, Clara Darling, and Melanie Morgan. You have always been the best of writing buddies, so sweet and supportive! And thank you, Bryn, for helping educate me on this crazy world of publishing.

Thank you to Rachelle Rae Cobb for being such an awesome editor! Your enthusiasm was a complete blessing.

Thank you to Anne Elisabeth, who first inspired me to write fairy tale retellings. Your example of beautiful excellence gave me a vision for my own aspirations.

And thank you, Rin, for creating such perfectly lovely illustrations of Idris and Keeva!

❧ About the Author ❧

From the beginning, H. S. J. Williams has loved stories and all the forms they take. Whether with word, art, or costume, she has always been fascinated with the magic of imagination. She lives in a real fantastical kingdom, the beautiful Pacific Northwest, with her very own array of animal friends and royally loving family. Williams taught Fantasy Illustration at MSOA. She may also be a part-time elf.

꧁ About the Artist ꧂

Irina Plachkova is an acclaimed artist, freelance illustrator, and fashion designer, better known as PhantomRin. You can find more of her work at phantomrin.tumblr.com.

Want to see the illustrations in color?

Visit the author's site at

www.hsjwilliams.com